NOT FAMOUS
in Hollywood

LEONIE GANT

ISBN-13: 978-0-9942990-4-8

Dedication

To my personal cheer squad: Mike, Samuel and Nicholas.
Thank you for making this dream possible.

Chapter One

In an ideal world there are mornings when the sun is warm, the coffee is hot and all the annoying people are tucked up in their own beds. I love those mornings. I live for those mornings. Unfortunately this is not one of those mornings. Instead, the air was cool, I hadn't had coffee, and thanks to one of those annoying people, I was stuck in a doggie door. Wedged in tight, thanks to hips that haven't seen size zero since before puberty.

Knowing that I was stuck, I stopped wriggling and wondered if I started banging my head against the tiled floor in the kitchen, whether anyone would notice. I really should have had a coffee before starting my day. With the cheap plastic frame of the door biting into my hips, I really wished that a crippling case of stage fright had not stood between me and my childhood dream of certain stardom in Hollywood. That and a complete lack of talent, oh, and not having the right figure, or the right look. Other than that I could have been a star.

I did make it to Hollywood. Unfortunately, thanks to Fate having a cruel sense of humor, I was not in Hollywood walking the red carpet for the premiere of my latest film, with a gorgeous, adoring leading man by my side.

Instead I came to Hollywood with the job title of personal assistant. Of course, like so many other things in Hollywood, that title isn't a true reflection of what I do. In reality I am a specialist in risk management, especially when it comes to people who are so self-absorbed that they don't see the upcoming cliff of disaster. I am hired, usually by the people who make money out of these stars, as an on the scene public relations disaster prevention specialist. That is a much more exciting job title, but unfortunately, not one that I am allowed to put on my business card. I am also unable to use babysitter to the spoiled and indulged, another job title that while accurate, could be interpreted as slightly unprofessional.

My job is to ensure that the star I've been assigned to doesn't go off the rails in a way which affects their brand or money earning potential, because that is what is important in this town. This usually entails me sticking by their sides from the moment they wake up until the moment they go to sleep. As a result I generally only do these jobs short term. Unfortunately my current job had been a little more involved than I had originally been expecting.

It had taken weeks of maneuvering to get my first day off in months. I'd had great plans for today. I hadn't quite worked out what those plans were yet, but number one was that they didn't comply with someone else's demands. Eleanor Channing's demands to be precise.

Everyone knows Eleanor Channing. Everyone loves Eleanor Channing. Not everyone has to live with Eleanor Channing and keep her real personality from reaching her adoring fans. That would be bad. That is where I come in. I work for an agency which deals with difficult clients. You see, there are always employers who have trouble keeping staff. This is where my boss saw an opportunity. Monique Petit worked in the Hollywood system for twenty years and learned that the good money is with those people who treat their staff like garbage.

Seeing an opportunity, Monique set up her own temporary staff recruitment agency and she prides herself on hiring only those people who are smart, diplomatic and have the patience of a saint. Or at the very least can bite their tongue, no matter how much they are provoked. Monique's people do not have screaming meltdowns on YouTube about their bosses. They don't tell all their friends on Facebook about the latest STD their client has, regardless of the provocation, and believe me when I say, the people I deal with specialize in provocation.

I am one of Monique's personal assistants. I'd been hired by Eleanor Channing's management to make sure that one of the world's biggest box office draws doesn't do something stupid, like show the world what she's really like, you know, self-absorbed, self-important and insecure. Her management needed help after her own sister, who was her previous assistant, did that meltdown on YouTube that I mentioned earlier. I've seen it and it was brutal. It was also hilarious. No one but family could do that much damage to the woman that had actually won awards for being Hollywood's most likable star. I downloaded it and I bring it out every now and then when she really pushes my buttons. Not for anyone else's enjoyment. I am one of Monique's people so that would be unprofessional. No, this is my secret guilty pleasure, kind of like those special romance books you have hidden in your bedside drawer. Nobody needs to know about it.

This brings me to how I ended up stuck in a doggie door, in a very nice house, in an exclusive part of LA, at the crack of dawn, on my only day off in months. Faced with not having me to run her life for a lousy twenty-four hours, Eleanor Channing decided to have a one night stand with her former boyfriend, Ryan Hendricks. Ryan Hendricks is a Hollywood bad boy who has made his name sleeping with just about every famous and not so famous actress in Hollywood. With his effortless good looks and everyman persona, Ryan Hendricks was seen as pretty much impossible to resist. Upon waking up, rather than performing the usual walk of shame, which in her case would be contacting the limo service, she called me, desperate to extricate her from the situation.

The main issue was that this particular Hollywood bad boy has supposedly reformed, and is now set on marrying the sweet innocent daughter of one of the studio heads. I saw the beautiful and touching story in the tabloids. Really, it was so beautiful, the story of how she tamed his wild ways. I would have been touched if I hadn't caught him that night, at a party, in a toilet with two women, while I was looking for Eleanor, in an effort to stop her from doing precisely what she did last night on my first day off. Look at that, I'm still angry.

Finding my way to the house was easy. Regrettably, this was not the first time I'd had to do this particular duty. My job requires me to perform a balancing act. My first goal is to head off any disasters before they happen. Unfortunately, these are adults we are talking about, even if they don't act like it, so sometimes the disaster is going to happen no matter what. If we have gone past the point of prevention, then I have to minimize the fallout. You would think that considering the entourages these people have, that there would be one person who would say stop, and perhaps suggest that maybe some thought might need to be put into the stupid move that was about to occur. In reality that doesn't happen. Entourages are made up of people whose livelihood depends on them agreeing with everything the star says. Not one person is willing to ask the star if they are freaking nuts. That would be my job.

So back to the reason for me being in this mess. I couldn't really blame Eleanor for running back to Ryan when he crooked his finger. The man is hot, he could get anyone to sleep with him. Not me of course. Considering his steady diet of actresses and models, there is no way I would allow this guy to look at my body in anything less than a nun's outfit. I don't think my ego would be able to handle the look of dismay. It's not that I am that objectionable to look at, but I am normal. It is one of my strengths as a Hollywood assistant. In a world full of beautiful people I am breathtakingly average. Average height, average brown hair, average gray eyes, average looks. These actresses can hire me and know that their husbands or boyfriends will not look at me as anything but a piece of furniture. When I walk into a room with them, I am as likely to be noticed as the plant in the corner. I am the ultimate bridesmaid, never outshining the bride.

I had been surprised when I arrived at the house to find the front gates open. I didn't even need to be buzzed in. That was unusual. I knew this wasn't Ryan's main house. That was a mansion in one of the more popular areas of Los Angeles. This was the house for extracurricular activities. It was a nice house behind a large fence, but it wasn't anything special. I think Ryan chose it because it was so nondescript.

Even though it wasn't his main house, I would normally expect to be almost indecently frisked by some freakishly huge bodyguard, who had a gigantic view of their own importance in the grand scheme of things. As you can see I don't have a great attitude to bodyguards either. I have been literally walked over by bodyguards when I have been in the way. Today however, the lack of staff was unusual. Most actors have an entourage and Ryan Hendricks had a big one. This man was not able to do anything for himself. That being said, his future father-in-law was one of the most important people in Hollywood and last night Ryan had cheated on his daughter. Again. Maybe Ryan was smarter than I gave him credit for and realized his stupidity did not need an audience.

After I'd parked my car in front of the house I dragged myself up the steps. I knocked on the front door. Actually, to be perfectly honest, I pounded on the front door. Listening intently, I couldn't hear any movement in the house, even when I kicked the door for good measure. I tried the doorknob in the vain hope the door had been left open for me but that would have made my day easy, and I knew from the moment my phone started ringing this morning, that easy was not going to be how this day went down.

Walking around the house, I tested doors and windows, all with no luck. I tried calling Eleanor on her phone, but of course she didn't answer. I really did not want to know why she wasn't answering.

While trying the kitchen door I spotted the doggie door. Now this was the point when bad decisions started to be made. The thing is, I looked at that doggie door and thought I'd be able to fit, no problem. It's all a matter of perception and my perception was that I could fit in that door if I went through on my side. Sometimes I forget that the difference between perception and reality can be vast. My perception is that I have a body that while not as slim as the clients I have in the acting industry, it is still small enough to slide through a doggie door for a decent sized dog. I mean it isn't like the door was built for one of those little dogs that fit in a handbag. This doggie door was big enough for a medium to large dog and I was trying desperately to remember if Ryan Hendricks actually owned a dog. With all the noise I'd been making, I would have thought, if there was a dog on the property, it would have already come out to attack me. My getting through that door. That was my perception.

Unfortunately, the reality was that last night I had chocolate cake with ice cream and I didn't exactly have a sliver of a slice. The word diet has never been one that I have found to be particularly well used in my vocabulary. That meant that although I barely managed to get the top half of my body through the door, I was now well and truly wedged at the hip level.

I had two options here. I could try to wriggle out again and give up, turn around and head home. I could pretend I'd been talking in my sleep when I answered the phone and had no memory of the conversation. My other alternative was to grab hold of something and wrench myself through the door. I seriously considered the talking in my sleep option for five full minutes but I knew that the woman would just keep calling until I got here. Of course then I heard the growling of a dog coming from outside the door. It seems that when I was walking around the dog that belonged to this door had seen me as too much of a threat. Now I was simply a butt and legs hanging out the door, the dog thought he could take me. I no longer had a choice.

With a healthy dose of panic, I wriggled around until my hips were lined up with the widest part of the opening. I placed my hands on the floor as if I was doing a forty-five degree push up, used my feet to push and my hands to pull myself through the door. As I felt my hips scraping against the hard edges of the plastic I heard a crashing noise as I hit the floor with the doggie door frame still wedged around my hips, splintered wood around what was now an uneven hole in the door. With a yelp the dog took off, obviously deciding that I had reached threat level again.

Grabbing hold of the brittle piece of plastic around my hips, I wiggled and bent until it hit the floor. Looking at the now mangled and broken remains of the doggie door, I knew that there was no way that it was ever going back in that door. Not much I could do about it now, and seriously, somebody should have answered the door to me, so it really wasn't my fault.

"Hello, Miss Channing," I called. "It's me, Trudie."

No answer. Not that I was hugely surprised. I headed upstairs towards the bedrooms. I'd been here before. Often. I knew where to go. Knocking on the bedroom door I prayed they weren't having sex. In fact as the door opened I could see that Eleanor was the only one sitting on the bed. Her shoulder length blonde hair was wet and strands were clinging to her face. Those blue eyes that more than one overenthusiastic critic had claimed you could drown in, were swimming with tears.

My gut clenched as I raced over to her. This was not what I was expecting to see.

"Are you okay?" I looked her over.

Regardless of how she treated me, if Ryan Hendricks had hurt her I was going to destroy him.

"I think I killed him," I heard her whisper.

"Where is Ryan?" I asked, hoping that I had misheard.

Eleanor looked over my shoulder at the bathroom where I could hear the shower was running.

Making my way towards the bathroom, I had a very bad feeling. Pushing open the door, I saw Ryan Hendricks's body slumped in the shower. Reaching in, I turned off the water. I couldn't see any blood or any reason for him to be like that. My first instinct was to check he was dead. He certainly looked dead, but if it was me lying there, I would want someone to make damn sure there wasn't a spark of life left in me. I knelt beside the former hottest man alive and tentatively placed my fingers against his neck. No pulse there. The chest didn't seem to be moving but I put my ear against it to see if I could hear anything at all. Nothing. I strode out of the bathroom.

"Are you hurt?" I asked Eleanor, looking her over as I pulled my cell out of my pocket. It had miraculously survived the doggie door incident.

I couldn't see any sign that she was actually hurt. She turned to me with her eyes glazed. I was hoping it was from shock and not some artificial stimulant. I grabbed her shoulders and shook her lightly. My first choice would have been slapping her, but considering I still had some residual anger at her for getting herself, and by extension me, into this situation, I couldn't be sure I could moderate that slap.

"Eleanor Channing," I said loudly and clearly. "I need you to tell me if you are hurt at all."

"No," she said softly, in an almost childlike voice, "but Ryan won't wake up."

That didn't sound like she was functioning on all cylinders. I knew about shock and drugs, I worked in the entertainment industry after all. I quickly dialed 911, informing the operator that I had a man who wasn't breathing. Once I got off the phone I turned my attention back to Eleanor who still had that glassy look in her eyes.

"It'll be alright," I said soothingly, lying through my teeth.

Nothing about this situation was going to be alright. Ryan Hendricks hadn't been a particularly pleasant human being, but for millions of women out there he represented the ultimate man of their dreams. He was going to be missed. Mostly by people who didn't actually know him, but he had family and friends. He had a fiancée who was going to be devastated. At this stage I looked at my phone and started dialing Monique's phone number. I quickly explained the situation to her and hung up. I know, I'm not too proud of the fact I was supposed to do that. We all read those stories of these kind of situations and judge the person who contacts a lawyer, a manager or the media in that moment. The fact of the matter was that I was in a volatile situation. This mess could go any number of different ways and dealing with it was way above my pay grade.

I heard a crash downstairs as the front door was kicked open and rebounded against the wall.

"We're up here," I yelled, as I grabbed Eleanor's shoulders and gently tried to pull her away from the bed.

Feet pounded up the stairs and two uniformed police officers came through the bedroom door, guns first. In that moment terror gripped me. I grew up in Australia, and though I'd been living in Los Angeles for six months, the fact that guns were so prevalent still terrified me. I didn't know where to look when a gun was pointed at me. I lacked the necessary etiquette for these situations.

"Freeze, don't move," the cops yelled out.

I was only too happy to comply. Finally someone was telling me what to do. I froze, but at that moment the Eleanor Channing that I knew and couldn't stand came screaming to the fore.

"How dare you!" she screeched. "Do you know who I am?" she said, walking unsteadily towards the police.

I was thinking that if she got too close to them she would be on the morning news as the late, not so great, actress Eleanor Channing. I would have lost my first client in one of the worst ways possible. Now that I think about it, there were worse ways for her to go out, but why did she have to do it on my watch.

"Ma'am, step back now or we will have to shoot," one of the police shouted.

She didn't. I didn't really expect her to. When you've been in the rarefied air where everyone is willing to give you anything you want, you start to think that the world really does revolve around you. The idea of being denied doesn't even come into your head. I expected Eleanor to keep haranguing the two poor cops about who she was. What I didn't expect was for one of them to grab his stun gun and shoot America's sweetheart. The look of surprise on her face as those two prongs hit her was priceless. I hoped they didn't leave a mark on her skin because then she would be really upset. She went down with a thud. My jaw dropped and though it was totally inappropriate, I fought the beginnings of a smile. The cop looked at me as if he couldn't quite believe what had just happened and I just shrugged my shoulders. Really, she brought it on herself.

Chapter Two

It is amazing how quickly a situation escalates when celebrities are involved. Paramedics arrived soon after the police. Once it was determined that there wasn't anything they could do for Ryan, they turned their attentions to Eleanor. I'd hoped that being stunned might at least induce, if not respect, maybe a little bit of fear of the law. As usual I was wrong. The second that woman was able to speak again, she did so loudly and without taking a breath.

Having seen the power of the stun gun I was not willing to say a word, so I just stayed in the background, trying desperately to be unnoticed. The couple of times when I did try to calm her down and suggest she wasn't doing herself any favors, I was swiftly told in no uncertain terms that my opinion was not wanted, and that unless I could get her out of here, then I was completely useless.

At that point I figured that I had done the best I could. I smiled apologetically to all the emergency workers in the room. All I could do now was to try and work out how we were going to deal with the fallout when footage of this little tirade ended up on some media show. Because it would. One thing I have learned is that people have an amazing capacity to hold a grudge. I have often been told that I am too nice, that I let people walk all over me. Despite that, I have to admit, seeing Eleanor stunned gave me a nice feeling, as if it was payback for all the insults and abuse that she had dealt to me over the last few months. I was sure that regardless of the professionalism of the people in this building, one of them had a recorder working on their cell phone and it was taking down every vile thing that Eleanor was saying. At some point that recording was going to find its way to the media.

So let's count down how bad this was going to be for Eleanor. First, she slept with a man that she knew was engaged. Next, her booty call died while she was in the building. She, and I knew this was how it was going to be written up in the police report, attacked two police officers responding to the scene and they were forced to subdue her by using a stun gun. Finally, she was abusing police, paramedics and the coroner, all hard working, salaried employees of the city. When all this hit the news circuit, every commentator was going to have a field day. I winced as I looked through the window and saw the media trucks pulling up outside of Ryan's house. This was so not good.

There were people everywhere bustling around us. The poor young officer who had been first on the scene was standing near me looking sick. He looked young, like he was playing dress up.

"Are you okay?" I asked, feeling a bit sorry for him.

He gulped in some air. "I just stunned Eleanor Channing." He had obviously only now started realizing the enormity of what he had done. There was no denying it. He had, and she went down like a sack of potatoes.

"I'm going to lose my job."

"Maybe not," I said sympathetically. "I think everyone here is going to say she deserved it."

The poor guy nodded gratefully but I could already see him mentally working out what career he might be better suited for.

"It could have been worse," I tried to say helpfully. "You could have shot her." The poor man didn't look convinced. I smiled at him. "If you want to focus on the positive side, you've given me a memory that I will treasure for the rest of my life."

He didn't look as if that helped him at all.

I watched as the paramedics loaded Eleanor into the ambulance. As she continued to berate them, I could only marvel at the level of self-control it must have taken not to tip over the stretcher and dump their complaining charge on the ground. As the ambulance pulled out there was a mad scramble amongst the media as they tried desperately to get photos of the inside of the vehicle. As it pulled through the throng some of the media vans chased after it, while others tried to make the call as to where the bigger story was.

I'd tuned out most of the voices around me. I seemed to have been forgotten and I was severely regretting not having a coffee this morning. Not to mention I hadn't eaten yet. I have a tendency to become a little cranky when I go without food. It's one of the reasons I don't diet. I'm not willing to inflict that part of my personality on my fellow man. That's my reasoning and I'm sticking to it. I was imagining how good the pecan pie that I had at home would taste right about now, when I realized someone was standing in front of me waiting for an answer. I blinked and discovered I hadn't seen these officers enter the premises. I had been so intent on ignoring everything that was happening around me that I had missed these cops. I should have noticed.

This is the reason why ordinary women in LA have it so hard. When the cops look like this. The male cop was hot but not in the pretty boy way that I was used to seeing in my industry. He was masculine and looked like he could chew nails and spit out bullets. Tall with dark short hair and green eyes, he looked hard and strong. His partner on the other hand was gorgeous. With her tanned skin and black hair she would have looked perfect on a fashion magazine, but no, this is LA where even the cops look like this. I didn't have a chance. No wonder my social life was so lackluster, well that and I worked for a tyrant who sucked the joy out of my life. Every. Single. Day. Maybe I should find another job. I was becoming remarkably bitter working for Eleanor.

"Sorry, I didn't catch that." I hoped I sounded cooperative. After Eleanor's continuous tirade I could only imagine the level of patience the police would have with me.

"Which part?" asked the female cop.

"Pretty much all of it," I replied. "I kind of zoned out a bit there."

"Really," the male cop said, and a part of me melted. He had a voice that was deep and just sort of caressed its way over me. "Not really smart considering you're at a murder scene."

And just like that he became a lot less attractive to me. My eyes narrowed.

"I'm sorry, it has been a trying morning and I was just doing my best to deal with a traumatic experience. How can I help you?" I asked, with just that extra dollop of sickening sweetness, all the while picturing his admittedly gorgeous head as a bowling ball. I could tell that they weren't sure how to deal with my change in attitude. I have discovered in LA that people are always prepared for abuse. They have a plan for it. Sometimes that plan includes a well placed put down, sometimes it is to be profane and at other times it is pulling the finger. In those situations being polite can completely throw them. They don't know how to respond and especially adding it to the blank facial expression where they can't read any cues, drives people nuts. My job requires that I be this way, and I excel at it. The female cop, obviously reading the cues that I was not impressed with her partner, took the lead.

"I am Detective Ramos of the LAPD, Homicide and this is Detective Griffin. We just want to know what happened."

"Well," I said, "I arrived here almost an hour ago. Miss Channing had called me to come and pick her up. I found the place locked but managed to get inside. I went upstairs looking for her. I found Miss Channing in the bedroom and Mr Hendricks in the shower. I turned off the shower and checked for signs of life. I then called 911."

All this was said very correctly and with no emotion at all.

Detective Griffin's eyes narrowed as he looked at me. "We found signs of a break-in downstairs," he said.

"If you're talking about the doggie door, that was me. A little accident while I was trying to get in."

"What did you do, try to fit through it?" Detective Ramos said.

I could feel myself tense up. Of course Detective Perfect Figure would have got through that door without a problem.

"Where was Miss Channing when this happened?" Griffin interrupted.

I stopped myself from swallowing nervously. This was the part that I knew was coming. I knew how the rest of this statement was going to look. I had no loyalty to Eleanor Channing and if she murdered Ryan Hendricks I would be the first to say she should get what was coming to her. The problem was that despite my personal feelings for the woman, I couldn't picture her as a murderer. That being said, I wasn't going to cover for her either. My mother didn't raise an idiot.

"Miss Channing was sitting on the bed when I arrived," I said softly. "She seemed to be in shock and didn't respond to anything I said. I checked to see if she had been hurt as well but I couldn't see anything." I spoke calmly and clearly.

"We will need to take your statement down at the station," Ramos said briskly. "Once Miss Channing has been checked out, we'll be talking to her as well." She indicated that I should follow and I fell into step behind the two of them.

I had to stop myself from laughing. They had no chance of speaking with Eleanor. By the time she got to the hospital, the fortress of lawyers, managers and entourage would be back in place and these cops wouldn't get anywhere near her. Unfortunately I didn't merit the same protection, so I would be left hanging in the wind until somebody worked out that I had some value in protecting Eleanor. Until that crucial moment I was on my own.

With that demoralizing thought, I pulled my hair out of the ponytail and let it hang forward as we drove through the property gates. Flashes went off around the car. The media had no idea who I was and I preferred to keep it that way. If I could keep my face hidden, maybe I could get through this without my family seeing my photo in a newspaper, with a headline proclaiming that I was a murderer.

Once at the station I followed Ramos and Griffin, and I swear I did not look at the way Detective Griffin filled out that pair of jeans once.

Hearing a yell I heard Griffin mutter, "what the hell this time?"

"The lieutenant wants to see the three of you," the young uniformed officer said.

Traipsing back to the lieutenant's office I was happy to see who was also there. My boss, Monique Petit. Monique, many years ago, was a model. She had come over to America from France, when she was young, to be an actress. But due to not being the right look, had not been able to find the roles that she wanted. Monique is a couple of inches over six feet tall and after all these years is still gorgeous. Her skin is a rich chocolate color and even though she is heading towards fifty she seems much younger. One look at the lieutenant's adoring face and I knew that he was going to be putty in Monique's hands. I had seen men on road crews move equipment so she could have a parking space, just for a smile from her. That kind of thing never worked for me.

Standing next to Monique was her husband, Reggie Goodman. Reggie adores Monique and he is the only person in the world who can manage her. Reggie is like me, completely ordinary. He is shorter than Monique, stocky and had started losing his hair at a young age. People never assume that the two of them are together and when they finally work it out, there is always that look as if they can't understand why she is with him. I know why. Reggie is one of the most wonderful and supportive men I had ever met in my life. Monique is very much aware of how lucky she is to have him.

The lieutenant obviously didn't realize that he was leering at Reggie's wife. Reggie may not look like he could do damage, but I have seen big tough guys cry once Reggie had got a hold of them. At this moment though, the important thing to me about Reggie is that he is an attorney, and not just any attorney. Reggie is brilliant. I've seen him in action and when he is passionate about something he can wipe the floor with anyone else. Usually he would be way out of my price range, but as a favor to Monique I was sure I would be getting the special rate. He also likes the fact that I can cook. When I am stressed I bake and so that I don't eat everything I make, I share the baked goods around. Reggie loves my chocolate and pecan cookies. I could see some big baking days in my future. Never underestimate the baking barter system. If you can make someone's favorite treat from when they were a kid, you have a friend for life.

Detective Griffin cleared his throat. "What can we do for you, Lieutenant?" he asked.

I looked at the man with newfound respect. Any man who can speak coherently when in the presence of Monique obviously has a level of self-control that approached legendary. I saw a flash of irritation cross Monique's face. Although she is happily married to Reggie and wouldn't think of straying, there is still a small part of her that is proud of her effect on men. To find a man that doesn't immediately fall under her spell pushes that competitive spirit button in her.

"Oh, uh, this is Miss Eyre's counsel," the lieutenant said, waving a hand at Reggie without actually taking his eyes off Monique.

"I assume that means we are not getting a statement,"

Griffin said, looking at me with his eyes narrowed.

The vindictive part of me that wasn't interested in making his life any easier was kind of on board with that. I was not looking forward to sitting in an interrogation room for hours while being good cop, bad copped by the beautiful twosome. There are better ways to spend my day. I had already told them what I'd seen.

I looked at Monique and Reggie. There is a reason I work for Monique. In a world where values and ideals are constantly compromised, she manages to follow the right path. She is devoted to a husband who may not be everyone's ideal in the way he looks, even though temptation is thrown her way all the time. She makes it clear to all her staff that despite the world they work in, where drugs and sex are freely traded, she expects us to conduct ourselves according to our moral compass. She was also a strong advocate of taking individual responsibility. Even though she was letting me make the choice, I knew she expected me to do the right thing. Regardless of what happened, Ryan Hendricks was dead. Though I didn't like the guy personally, if someone else was responsible for his death, he deserved justice.

"I'll make a statement," I said, looking Griffin directly in the eyes.

I could see he was surprised, and maybe it was just my imagination, but I thought I saw a flash of respect go through them.

"I will be going in with her," stated Reggie.

I smiled at him gratefully and mentally promised him a double batch of chocolate and pecan cookies. As the four of us headed to the interrogation room, Monique stopped me and pulled me into a quick hug.

"Be smart, listen to Reggie, and I'll see you when you are finished," she murmured, before striding through the room with every man watching her leave.

"I need to speak to my client alone before we do this," said Reggie.

Detective Ramos pointed him to an empty room and Reggie grabbed my hand and pulled me forward. I noticed the way the two detectives took note of the familiar move. I didn't care. Reggie was like that with me all the time. He liked to call me the younger sister he never wanted and our relationship reflected that.

Once in the privacy of the room, Reggie turned to me. "Did you do anything that I should know about?"

"Of course not, Reggie," I said indignantly. "I got there after a phone call from Eleanor and found him dead. I have no idea what happened before then. I called 911 and then I called Monique, after checking to see if Ryan was still alive."

"Please tell me you didn't touch the body," Reggie said.

"I checked his pulse, that's it," I said.

"Alright then," said Reggie. "Let's get this done. When we are in there I want you to think before you speak. Don't run off at the mouth. Don't feel intimidated. I will be with you through this entire thing." He squeezed my hand and I felt tears prick the back of my eyes.

"For the love of God, don't cry," he said hurriedly.

"I'm not," I said, sniffing loudly. "You're just being nice to me, I've had four months with Eleanor Channing. I'm just not used to nice. It's throwing me off my game."

"Very well," Reggie said. "I'll be a bastard for the rest of the day. Don't worry, if someone being nice to you is what makes you cry, you should be fine for the rest of this meeting. I don't think Griffin and Ramos are going to be particularly pleasant with you."

"I think you could be right," I agreed.

Chapter Three

Sitting in the interrogation room, I started once again questioning why I was doing this. Ramos started the interview and I could feel myself sweating as Reggie droned on about my rights and how I was doing them a favor. Ramos kept looking at him while Griffin kept his implacable stare on me. I couldn't help wondering what he was thinking and tried to meet his expression with my own tough glare, as if this whole situation didn't terrify me. I don't think it worked too well as the irritating man quirked his eyebrow at me and looked like he was having to stop himself from laughing.

"Thank you, Mr Goodman." Detective Ramos finally broke in when it looked like Reggie was about to recite the Constitution to them. "I think we can get started, a few details first. Can the witness please give us her name."

"Trudie Eyre." I was quite proud that there was only a small waver in my voice.

"Is that your full, correct name?" she asked with a small smile.

Great, she knew. I could tell from the look on her face that she knew that my mother had given me a name no modern mother should give their child.

"My full name is Gertrude Mary Eyre," I said, glaring at her.

I know, Gertrude. I was named after my dad's grandmother. To this day I don't understand what my mom was thinking. She says my great-grandmother was sick when I was born and they didn't know if she would live. Between that, the really long labor, the drugs and the pressure from my grandmother, she signed the paperwork without really thinking.

Once the situation had calmed down enough that she realized what she had done to her firstborn child, it was too late. The best she could do was shorten it to Trudie. That and tell me at least it wasn't a stripper name. No, I had a name as far from a stripper name as it was possible to get. A name that was pretty much guaranteed to be accompanied by the sentence, 'why would your mother do that' by everyone who heard it. I could tell that was the next question Detective Ramos wanted to ask, but she was a professional. She only looked like she wanted to burst out laughing at my stupid name. She didn't actually do it. I wasn't even game to look at Griffin. That quirking eyebrow of his made me want to slap him. Despite my limited knowledge of the American justice system, I'm pretty sure slapping a detective quirking an eyebrow at you because of the stupid name your mother gave you, would be considered a bad thing.

"You are not an American citizen are you?" she asked.

"No I'm not, I'm Australian," I said, sighing.

I knew where this was going. The one thing about working in America but not actually being an American, is that there are some people who assume you are here illegally. If you do anything that annoys them, or if they want something from you, they threaten to report you to Immigration.

"Miss Eyre is working in this country legally. I have all the paperwork here," Reggie interrupted, reaching into his briefcase.

Lucky for me Reggie did all my original paperwork, as Monique was the one who sponsored me for my green card. Ramos and Griffin weren't interested in the paperwork. I knew that and Reggie knew that. The question was just aimed to rattle my cage, make me feel uncertain about my status and a little bit more willing to cooperate. What they failed to realize was I had no idea about my status and the only reason I was holding it together was because Reggie was sitting beside me and his knee kept bumping my leg in what I think was a desperate attempt at communicating with me in Morse code. Unfortunately for me, I had no idea how to interpret what he was trying to tell me.

"Miss Eyre," Detective Griffin said with a smile.

I looked at him and the ingratiating expression was so far away from irritated or amused at my expense, that I did a double take. Okay so he was going to try to be good cop. Didn't look like he was comfortable with it. I tried to quirk my eyebrow at him, and if the expression on Ramos's face was anything to go by, it didn't work for me either.

"Can you tell us what happened this morning?" he asked.

I breathed in and tried to be smart, just like Monique told me. Lucky for me, Monique always gets me to write up any incidents with clients in a report format. She said in the litigious world that we lived in, we had to protect ourselves. I decided to approach this situation like I would one of those reports.

"Today was supposed to be my day off. My cell woke me this morning and it was Miss Channing. She informed me that she was at Mr Hendricks's house and wanted me to pick her up. I reminded Miss Channing that it was my day off and she should contact a limo service, who would be happy to pick her up. Miss Channing informed me that she paid me so my life was not my own, and that I better get my lazy ass out of bed or she would make sure I would never get a job in this town again."

At this point Reggie's knee was starting to leave bruises on my legs so I wasn't sure if he was happy with the level of detail I was giving. I was tired and cranky and these detectives were annoying me. Between Ramos looking like she wanted to laugh at me and Griffin quirking that damned eyebrow, I was not in the mood to answer questions. Seriously, I was wondering if it was a nervous tic.

"I got in my car and drove to Ryan Hendricks's house.

There were no staff in attendance which was unusual, as the man was not able to have a thought in his head without somebody putting it in there. I called out for Miss Channing but didn't receive an answer. I crawled through the doggie door as Miss Channing had neglected to leave a door open for me and wasn't answering when I knocked. I went upstairs to Mr Hendricks's bedroom and found Miss Channing sitting on the bed. She told me Mr Hendricks was in the bathroom. I went in the bathroom, as Miss Channing was distressed, and found Mr Hendricks slumped in the shower. I ascertained whether I could see any signs of life in Mr Hendricks, could not find a pulse and then I called 911."

I looked at Reggie, quite proud of myself. A good report I thought. Succinct and straight to the point.

"How did you know where Mr Hendricks's bedroom was?" asked Griffin.

"I've accompanied Miss Channing to several parties in that house before and know where most of the rooms are," I replied.

"Did Miss Channing and Mr Hendricks have a sexual encounter last night?" asked Ramos.

"You would need to ask Miss Channing that," I said, reaching for the glass of water in front of me.

Reggie beamed at me and I had a little smile myself. I was quite proud of myself for that answer. I'm pretty sure they went at it like bunnies last night but I don't know for sure, and these two police officers weren't going to trip me up with speculation. No way, I was on to them. I watch enough cop shows to be smart about this.

"Were you involved in a sexual encounter with Mr Hendricks last night?" Griffin asked.

He really should have waited until I'd finished that sip of water because I choked and sprayed a mouthful of it all over his shirt. Griffin jumped up and Reggie helpfully thumped my back as if I was choking to death. The man may be small but he has a strong arm on him.

"What?" I spluttered, tears running down my face as I desperately tried to get back control of my airways.

Griffin got back in his chair, trying to ignore the fact that I had just spewed water over him. At least it stopped him from quirking that eyebrow.

"I asked if you had a sexual encounter with Mr Hendricks last night?" he repeated.

"No," I said.

The two detectives waited, but I was no longer in a sharing mood.

"Have you ever had a sexual encounter with Ryan Hendricks?" Griffin ventured.

"No," I repeated.

Ryan Hendricks was gorgeous, there was no doubt about it. Despite my bravado and the fact I knew what his personality was like, if he had looked in my direction I am not so sure that I would have had the intestinal fortitude to say no. I hope so, but there is still that geeky teenage girl in me, the one who wouldn't mind being able to say I'd caught the attention of Ryan Hendricks. I'm not particularly proud of that facet of my personality, but there you have it. The fact of the matter was that I hadn't caught his attention.

"Have you ever had a sexual encounter with Eleanor Channing?" asked Ramos.

"Definitely not," I answered, the horror obviously evident in my voice. I have a friend who repeatedly says that all women are about three drinks from a girl on girl encounter. This friend is also a bit of a pig when it comes to women so it may be just his wishful thinking. If that statement is true though, to get me near Eleanor Channing, it would take a lot more than three drinks.

"Exactly where are you going with these questions?" Reggie asked, a bit too mildly for my tastes. Personally I would have preferred him to jump up, defend my honor, and demand apologies for the inappropriate questioning, but it looks like chivalry isn't what it used to be.

"Just trying to ascertain the nature of Miss Eyre's relationship with all parties involved," Griffin replied, just as mildly.

I narrowed my eyes at him. Yeah, I really didn't like him. I started doing my own Morse code thing with my knee against Reggie's leg. I wanted out of here now. Fortunately for me, Reggie is smarter than most people and he was able to translate my leg spasms into 'get me the hell out of here'.

"I think we're done here, Detectives. You have your statement. My client is the only person involved who actually tried to help the victim. If you have any other questions for her, please contact my office."

Reggie started packing his briefcase, indicating the interview was over.

As we were leaving Griffin cleared his throat. "We will be processing your car as it is part of the crime scene. We'll get it back to you when we can."

I turned around and Griffin quirked that damn eyebrow of his and tossed in a smirk just to get to me. Reggie, seeing that I was about to lose it, very wisely grabbed my arm and dragged me out of the station, all the time murmuring in my ear.

"Don't even think about it."

He got me into his car and once the doors were closed and he was sure we were alone, he turned to me.

"They are just trying to upset you. At the moment you are a witness, they can't really push you that much. The second you do something they will lock you up and interrogate you a lot harder than that."

"I wasn't going to do anything," I said calmly, staring straight ahead.

"Right," said Reggie. "You didn't want to hit that cop at all."

"I would never…" I spluttered.

"No of course not," said Reggie. "That's not like you at all."

I looked sideways at him and gave him my haughtiest expression. That didn't even deserve a response.

Chapter Four

Reggie dropped me off at the front of my apartment. As usual Miss Betsy was working in the gardens. Miss Betsy Peterman owned the entire complex and rented out the various apartments, generally to people that she felt were interesting. She liked to talk, but most of all she liked to listen and hear stories that people from different countries and different walks of life could bring her. After trying to find a reasonably priced place in LA, I'm sure I only landed this one because I launched into a story about the time I got chased by an emu when holidaying in the outback with my family when I was a kid. I wish it hadn't been true. Despite the fact she owned a very pricey piece of real estate in LA and was raking in the rent, she liked to do the maintenance on the building herself. It was not unusual to see Miss Betsy pottering around the place, her gray hair in a messy bun and with a tool belt around her hips. I always felt guilty when anything in my unit needed to be repaired and generally stayed there to do any of the heavy lifting. That being said, when she fixed something she did it well. She said she had to considering the bum of a husband she had tossed out on his rear years ago.

As I walked through the door to my apartment my cell phone rang insistently. Stupidly I didn't check caller ID before answering.

"Where are you?" screeched the familiar voice of Miss Eleanor Channing.

"Well, Miss Channing. I have just been dropped off at my home after spending the morning being questioned by the police."

"Why were they questioning you?" she asked suspiciously.

I looked at the phone and contemplated smacking it against my head. "They required a witness statement regarding the passing of Mr Hendricks earlier today," I said, wondering if she had actually forgotten.

"I know," she sighed. "It has been such a trauma for me. I need you to get here right now and take me to the spa so I can deal with everything I have been through."

"Actually, Miss Channing, I can't get to you right now. The police have impounded my car as it is considered to be a part of the crime scene. Maybe it would be a good opportunity for you to speak to your therapist and I will be there tomorrow morning to help you."

See, that's what you call self-control. Remember, this was still supposed to be my day off. Eleanor needs to be led to the next person to take care of her. She can't have a moment of the day where someone isn't holding her hand. Her entourage of managers, lawyers, hangers-on and I generally play a game of pass the starlet. She gets too much for one, we pass her along to the next person in the line.

Once I got Eleanor off the phone, I called her manager immediately. Eleanor at a loose end is a disaster waiting to happen, but for the rest of today she was somebody else's disaster. Of course there were no queries about how I had done at the police station. To be perfectly honest though, the guy probably didn't even know my name. I was just minion number one.

Flopping down on the couch I wrapped my arms around one of the cushions and promptly fell asleep. Next thing I heard was pounding on my front door. Not nice, polite knocking, no, this was pounding. Getting up from my couch I threw the cushion down and ripped open the door to find Detective Griffin about to assault it again.

"Not you again," I groaned. "What do you want now? I told you everything I know and weren't you supposed to speak to Reggie if you needed anything else?"

"Sorry, Miss Eyre," he said. "I'm not here with any more questions, I'm just returning your car. We've finished with it now and I knew it would be important to you to get it back." He smiled and I could swear I heard angels sing.

"You're being nice," I said, squinting up at him, still not fully awake. "Stop it, it doesn't suit you."

"I can be nice," he said, lowering his voice seductively.

I felt that butterfly feeling in the pit of my stomach, but then I stopped myself and thought this through. Detective Hottie was being pleasant and seductive to me, breathtakingly average me. I saw his partner. If she was his version of normal I had no chance. I know it sounds like I have low self-esteem. I prefer to think of it as a very strong grasp of reality. Detective Griffin and I had known each other for a total of eight hours at most, not nearly enough time for him to be seduced by my stellar personality. Seeing as I wasn't a big proponent of love at first sight, the whole seductive voice thing was just not working for me.

I reached for the keys that he was dangling in his hand. "Thank you very much."

He pulled the keys just out of my reach. "Any chance of getting a drink, I'm kind of warm at the moment. The air conditioning in your car doesn't work very well."

"The air conditioning works fine. It isn't my fault if you weren't able to turn it on," I said.

He quirked that eyebrow and had an expectant look on his face.

"Fine," I ground out, years of my mother's social etiquette indoctrination unable to be repressed. "Come in and you can have a drink."

I led him to the kitchen, opened the fridge, and tossed him a bottle of water. He looked at the bottle and then at me.

"You want anything else there's a grocery store around the corner," I told him, opening my own bottle.

He raised the drink to his lips, took a good couple of swallows and leaned against the kitchen counter. My apartment is a normal size but Detective Griffin managed to make it seem small.

"So, Detective Griffin," I said. "Why are you really here? Somehow I don't think returning my car, especially this quickly, is a high priority for the LAPD. Something tells me that there is a little more behind this visit."

"I'd like you to call me Jake," he said.

I cocked my head. "I don't think so, Detective Griffin. You have thirty seconds to tell me what you want or I'm calling Reggie to say you're harassing me, and believe me that man would like nothing better than making your life difficult. He likes my cookies."

"Really," said Griffin with a smirk on his face.

"I mean he likes the cookies I make, chocolate chip with pecans. They're really good and I make them for him. In fact that's what I should be doing now, so get out so I can start."

I'd lost control. I knew it and Griffin knew it.

"Look I'm sorry," said Griffin. "This isn't normally my thing but we're getting stonewalled by Ryan Hendricks's people and Eleanor Channing's people. The lieutenant's a fan so he's not backing us up. I was hoping that you would have more information, maybe with your attorney not being around. None of what you say to me at the moment is admissible in court. We just need to get a handle on it."

"What is it you want to know?" I asked.

I was starting to feel a bit sorry for him. I could understand the frustration. My uncle is a cop back home in Australia so I kind of have a soft spot for the police. It's a thankless job, made more difficult by lawyers and people who don't believe the same rules apply to them that apply to the rest of us. Griffin ran his hand through his hair, frustration evident in the tense way he was holding himself.

"Is there anything else you can tell us? None of this can be used in court so rumors, information about the people involved, anything. You're involved in that world in a way we can't be. Surely there are things you've heard or seen that can help."

"Okay," I said. "Ask me what you want and I'll give you what I can."

"You are Eleanor Channing's personal assistant. What does that mean and what access does that give you?" he asked.

"Technically I work for Monique Petit. Eleanor Channing's management have contracted Monique's firm to provide a personal assistant. This gives me more freedom than most personal assistants have because I do not work for Eleanor. I can make choices on situations without being pressured by the client. Monique allocates me to clients who have had staffing issues previously."

"I'm guessing they have staffing issues because they are unpleasant to work for," Griffin put in.

"Got it in one, Detective." I saluted him with my water bottle.

"You would need to have a certain type of personality to cope with that kind of job," Griffin said. "I've dealt with some of the more difficult celebrities. I couldn't do that for longer than a few minutes at a time before doing some damage. How did you get the job?"

"I was recruited by Monique," I said.

"How?" asked Griffin.

"I was working in London as a nanny, short term jobs mostly. I was given a job for a musician who had his three year old daughter with him in a fancy hotel suite. Turned up and the guy was present but not completely accounted for, if you know what I mean. The regular nanny, who was also the personal assistant, had walked out on him, due to having to share the suite with him, the child and several groupies. The place was a mess and the kid was really unhappy. It was just a bad situation. I tried to sort out a small area for the daughter to be safe and then started cleaning. I contacted Monique, whose number I had found, as she was the assistant's boss. Monique turned up at the same time as the musician's wife. She was some strung out model, who went crazy when she found him in bed with the groupies. To complete the disaster his manager and the band mates arrived. Chaos was going on around me and I'm in a small play area I made with the little girl having a tea party. I remember singing to her, trying desperately to ignore the disaster that was this child's life. When it was finished, the little girl was packed off to her grandmother and I was making my escape. Monique approached me and offered a job. When I asked her why, she said I provided a place of calm that protected the child. She believed another person would have caved. I started working for Monique with a couple of clients in Europe and then I moved over here to take some jobs. After a couple of months I ended up with Eleanor. I'm not just her PA. I'm also supposed to keep her safe and grounded when everyone else in the world is telling her she isn't answerable to anyone. Sometimes I'm successful. Other times not so much."

"That sounds like more than a full time job," Griffin noted.

"It is. I've worked for Eleanor for four months now and today was supposed to be my first day off."

Griffin grinned.

"It's the reason I usually take short term jobs. This one has gone a bit longer than it was supposed to."

"What is Eleanor Channing like?" Griffin asked.

"Miss Channing is a woman of her environment," I said. "She makes money for everyone around her so they are not going to do anything that upsets her. Imagine if everyone around you told you that you were wonderful all the time, that you were beautiful all the time and that anyone who said anything against you was just being jealous. You'd get a pretty skewed view of the world wouldn't you?"

"I guess so," he replied.

"Well that's Eleanor Channing."

"You sound like you feel sorry for her," Griffin said.

"I do, kind of. It's hard to get past the fact that she's

gorgeous and talented and rude and drives me crazy sometimes, but she's also really alone. If she questioned the motives of all the people around her and why they claim to be friends with her, I think she'd find herself in a really dark place. I guess it's easier to be outrageous and demanding," I reflected.

Looking up, I saw Griffin's face had softened.

"What?" I asked.

"You sound like a nice person," he said, only mildly surprised. "Not many people are that forgiving or understanding."

"Oh don't get me wrong," I replied. "I bitch and moan about her all the time because she does, on occasion, make my life into a living hell. I am seriously looking forward to the last day I see her and on principle, I will never shell out my hard earned money to watch her on the screen. That being said, I don't hate her or anything."

Griffin nodded. "Since you spend so much time with her I would think that you attend events and parties."

"All the time," I replied, taking a sip of water.

"Must be fun," Griffin commented.

"My own little circle of hell," I replied.

"Really," he remarked. "Any reason why?"

"You need to understand, none of these people are my friends, none of them like me and if you asked the next day, none of them would be able to place me. My job is to be unmemorable. I am there to make sure nothing happens that can embarrass Eleanor or, more importantly, damage the brand. If anyone remembers me then I have done something that takes attention away from her and in my world that is a bad thing. One of my biggest strengths in this business is I am so unmemorable. I do not take attention away from the beautiful people."

"You seem pretty memorable to me," Griffin said.

I looked at him sourly. "I'm already helping, you don't need to lay it on so thick."

"Don't take a compliment well do you," he

commented. "What about Ryan Hendricks? Was this hookup something recent?"

"You really cannot be that clueless," I said.

"What do you mean?" he asked.

It was times like these that I wondered about people who lived normal lives, where the minutiae of celebrity lives weren't as accessible as breathing.

"I am going to tell you what I know, but this is all before I started working for Eleanor, so it comes from tabloid magazines and gossip columns. About a year ago Eleanor and Ryan were pretty hot and heavy together. They were the big couple around town, seen at all the parties, premieres, everywhere. Then something happened. Rumor was Ryan cheated on her and they broke up. About six months ago Ryan started seeing Emily Saunders who is the daughter of Henry Saunders."

At Griffin's clueless expression I knew I needed to fill him in further. "Henry Saunders is head of one of the big movie production companies. He is very, and I mean very, powerful in this town. Ryan and his daughter were engaged which gives Ryan's career a boost. Makes Ryan pretty much untouchable."

"So if Ryan is engaged, what was he doing with Eleanor Channing?" Griffin asked.

"I wasn't there," I said, slowly and directly, "but I am assuming that Eleanor got a booty call. I left her at her home around ten last night. She and Ryan must have hooked up at some point after that. He would most likely have picked her up, because screwing around on Henry Saunders' daughter is not something you want to advertise. Limo drivers talk and Eleanor does not drive herself anywhere. She finds it too stressful and stress ages you."

"Would cheating on his fiancée be something that Ryan would do only once, or would it be more of a permanent character flaw?" Griffin asked.

"For that man it was something that came as naturally as breathing. In the last four months I have walked in on

Ryan Hendricks many times having sex with any number of women, sometimes multiple women."

"Any reason that you keep walking in on him, or would it just be a stalker issue?"

"Oh you think you are funny don't you?" I said humorlessly.

Griffin smiled at me. He had a really nice smile when it wasn't that horrible smirk thing he did. I mentally slapped myself. No falling for the gorgeous cop who is just using you for inside information.

"When I started working with Eleanor it was made clear to me that her hooking up with Ryan Hendricks would be very bad for her career. It was also made clear to me that she may not be completely over Ryan and so may be vulnerable to some seduction on his part. Part of my job was to try to prevent this from happening. They party in the same circles and sometimes I have needed to track down one or the other when they have slipped away from the party. That is why I knew where Ryan Hendricks's bedroom was. He holds a lot of parties there and if I lose track of Eleanor I have accidentally wandered into his bedroom pretending to be lost, to make sure the woman with him hasn't been Eleanor. I have also wandered into toilets, out in the garden, in closets and pretty much everywhere else in that house. I have seen a lot of actors and actresses in many varied sexual positions. Ryan Hendricks has figured prominently in these situations."

"So he hasn't been faithful to Emily Saunders," Griffin confirmed.

"Ryan Hendricks and faithful aren't anywhere close to being in the same time zone," I nodded.

"And yet you are saying that you have never had sex with Ryan Hendricks," Griffin said.

Okay, I was getting annoyed. "Seriously, you're going to start that again. Ryan Hendricks only needed to look in a woman's direction and she dropped her panties. I saw it again and again and we are talking about beautiful women who are unattainable to most of the male population."

"But he never looked in your direction?"

"No he didn't."

"Did that upset you in any way?"

"No it didn't. I never expected Ryan Hendricks's attention and I never received it. Most of the times I saw him he was in various stages of undress with other women. He treated women like disposable objects and I would hope that my self-esteem was not so low that I would have been one of those women. And thanks to that line of questioning, your time is now up. Please leave my home."

Something in my demeanor obviously convinced Detective Griffin that I was serious and he straightened up to leave.

As we got to the door he turned. "Thank you for talking to me, Trudie. I do appreciate it. I have one more question though. Do you think Eleanor Channing could have killed Ryan Hendricks?"

"I personally don't think so," I replied, "but I really don't know."

With that I closed the door. How did I end up helping the cops anyway? I really needed to learn how to say no.

Chapter Five

There was a knock on the door.

"For goodness sake, I am done helping you," I yelled as I ripped open the door, only to find two of my neighbors standing there.

"Sorry," said Crystal. "We waited for the hot guy to leave and we have pizza."

Edwin waved the box under my nose to underscore them inviting themselves.

"Sorry about that, I thought you were the cops again."

Crystal and Edwin made their way into my home and settled themselves in as if they spent all their free time there, which to be perfectly honest, they did.

"What has happened?" asked Crystal. "I saw you on the news feed being put in a cop car."

So much for hoping I wouldn't be recognized.

"Heard Ryan Hendricks shuffled off the mortal coil," Edwin added. "Let me guess. You finally had sex with him and it was too much for him and he died."

I rolled my eyes in exasperation. Crystal and Edwin are my neighbors and pretty much the only friends I have made since coming to LA. Crystal Bronstein works for her father who is one of the biggest casting agents in LA. Her mum was a Las Vegas showgirl who was married to her dad just long enough to give Crystal her name and receive a large alimony payment. Crystal stands barely above five feet but has a personality that enters a room before she does. Crystal loves old Hollywood glamour. Her clothing echoes the silhouette fashions of the thirties and forties, and she has the curvy figure which matches those classic looks perfectly. She and I bonded over a love of cookies and nights at home watching old movies.

Unfortunately her dad's job means that Crystal has to

get out a lot. Being one of the big casting agents in town, she is also always being squired to these social events by young, hopeful, gorgeous actors who are looking for that big break. Anyone who says becoming a star is about luck has no idea of the lengths some people go to. People do their research. Crystal has become the queen of accidental hookups. The number of times one of these actors has accidentally bumped into her and started a conversation is ridiculous. I once asked her if it bothered her the number of men she went out with that were just using her to meet her father. She just shrugged at me and said she was using them just as much.

Edwin Litchfield was the other friend I had made while in LA. Edwin was tall, blond, muscular and with that upper class English accent that makes women melt. He used to work as a model and then decided to be an actor. While waiting for his big break, he took any other job that he could. At the moment he was working as a personal trainer/lifestyle coach. He has the ability to makeover a woman from zero to fabulous in no time flat. Considering his two closest friends were women he also set off every gaydar in a five block radius. This worked well for him as his clientele consisted of the bored housewives of the very rich in LA. Husbands were comfortable leaving their wives with a gay personal trainer. Unfortunately for those husbands, Edwin was one hundred percent straight and was very good at keeping a woman happy. He didn't advertise that fact but there were many women around LA who had enjoyed his company. Somehow none of them were bitter when he moved on. To this day I have no idea how he does it. Even after a one night stand he manages to meet up with a woman years later and they still think he is wonderful. Neither I nor Crystal have partaken of the irresistible nature that is Edwin. I think that may be why he is so comfortable with us.

"So," Edwin said, jamming a slice of pizza in his mouth. "What happened? So far we've seen you and

Eleanor Channing through blurry telephoto lens pictures. Eleanor being carted away in an ambulance and you in a police car, after Ryan Hendricks was found dead. Crystal called me and we rushed home to find out what was going on, only to find some hottie waiting at your front door." He grinned.

"You know Edwin," I said. "There are reasons people think you are gay. Calling other men 'hottie' is one of those reasons."

At that point cheese and tomato sauce slid off Edwin's slice of pizza and landed on his chest. He licked the stain, sucking the excess sauce out of his shirt, shrugged and got back to what he was eating.

"And that is why we know you are straight," murmured Crystal.

The two of them looked at me expectantly.

"Eleanor called me this morning so she didn't have to do the walk of shame. I got there and found Ryan Hendricks dead."

"Oh my God," exclaimed Crystal. "You actually saw the body. That is the coolest thing ever."

Edwin and I stopped eating and looked at her.

Realizing how she must sound, she quickly amended. "No, I don't mean that. Ryan Hendricks being dead is not cool, but you finding him, that is so cool. Trust me, you are going to be able to use that story forever," she said brightly.

"Great," I muttered. "That makes up for the trauma of it all."

"Oh, are you traumatized?" Crystal reached over and laid her hand on mine in sympathy. "I know this great therapist who will be able to help."

Just what I needed, therapy. I really didn't feel like I needed to go down that road at all.

"I'm fine," I said.

Actually thinking about it, I was fine. I'd got so caught up in everything that happened that I hadn't even registered that I had seen an actual dead body. I better put that thought away or I was going to need Crystal's therapist. Denial, everyone's best friend. Now Edwin and Crystal were looking at me carefully. The last thing I needed was for them to start worrying about me.

"Really, I'm fine," I said. "I was more worried about Eleanor, she was the one who was there."

"Did she kill him?" Edwin asked, his eyes gleaming.

"Really?" I said. "That would please you, that Eleanor Channing killed Ryan Hendricks."

"Not pleased exactly," said Edwin, only looking slightly shamefaced. "I'm just saying that as far as possible stories go, that would be the best one. Ryan Hendricks dumps Eleanor Channing, gets engaged to Emily Saunders and then during a passionate tryst with Eleanor she kills him with a ... gun?" His voice raised at the end in question.

"I have no idea. I couldn't make out any wounds on the body," I said.

"See the information you have. Do you realize how much money you could make going to the media with this, like right now?" Edwin said. "First on the scene after Eleanor Channing kills Ryan Hendricks after sex. It's got the whole black widow thing going for it."

"I am not going to the media," I said. "The police are dealing with it. My doing an interview is just going to make it harder to find if anyone killed Ryan. Anyway I don't believe Eleanor did it."

"Really," said Crystal. "I seem to recall you telling us the other day that the woman was evil and you wouldn't be surprised if she actually killed somebody one day."

"Okay yes, she is pure mean when she wants to be, and yes, her track record with men and the way she has tried to get back at them does indicate some sociopath tendencies."

I winced thinking of the words she had scratched on one ex-boyfriend's car after he dumped her. That may have been one of those rumors that Detective Hottie, I mean Griffin, would have wanted to hear about. Eleanor just sometimes came a bit unhinged when it came to boyfriends, and due to her complete lack of musical talent, she was unable to decimate their reputations in song in classic, malicious ex-girlfriend tradition. So Eleanor fell back on tried and true methods. Stalking, destroying careers and vandalism of property. Maybe I was wrong in believing she hadn't gone one step further and actually killed one of them. The more I thought about it, the more it seemed likely that it could happen. I realized I had been thinking too hard when I noted the silence around me.

"Oh no," said Edwin. "You think she might have done it."

I shook my head slowly. "I don't know. I was so sure she hadn't. She looked so shocked and upset when I found them."

Thinking back to this morning I froze.

"What is it?" asked Crystal.

"I forgot," I said. "When I got there Eleanor said she thought she'd killed him. I didn't think about it because she was pretty out of it but what if it was a confession?"

"Where was the body?" asked Edwin.

"In the shower. It looked like Eleanor had just come out of the shower too. Her hair was all wet," I said, biting my lower lip as I tried to remember anything else.

"Maybe they were having a shower together and he died then. It just might be one of those things people say," Crystal said.

"Or she may have done away with him while seducing him in the shower." Seemed like Edwin was keen to pin the crime on Eleanor.

"I thought for sure something else had to have happened," I said, twisting my napkin nervously. "But who am I kidding? There were only two of them there."

"Are you sure?" asked Crystal. "Could there have been anyone else in the house?"

"Well it is a decent sized house. I didn't see any cars

driving away. I guess there could have been someone else hiding there. I called 911 pretty much straight away and they were there in just a few minutes."

"Did you talk to Eleanor at all before the cops got there?" Crystal asked.

"No, she was almost catatonic, couldn't seem to answer any questions. The only time she said anything was when the cops arrived and they started ordering her around. She came out of it but then they stunned her and we were separated. What?" I asked as I saw the dropped jaws and looks on both Crystal and Edwin's faces.

"Eleanor Channing was stunned?" Edwin whispered in awe. "And you're not taking that information to the media?"

"No I'm not and everything I told you has to stay between us."

There were complaints to that statement because on a city run on gossip, the three of us were now sitting on gold.

"I mean it," I said, trying very hard to keep my stern face on.

My two friends looked so crestfallen that I knew how hard it was for them. I also knew they wouldn't tell anyone. That was the way we worked. The three of us all worked in areas where information was key. We were all privy to information that the tabloids would kill for. Being able to share that with each other and most importantly knowing that it would go no further was a major part of our friendship. That being said, I could tell that not being able to share this was almost going to kill them.

Chapter Six

Heading to Eleanor's the next morning, I wasn't feeling quite as refreshed as I had hoped to be after my supposed day off. After Crystal and Edwin had left, I had written up a detailed report on everything that had happened that day and emailed it to Monique. I decided not to include the follow up friendly visit from Griffin, just that the LAPD had delivered my car to me at home. I also notified her that I would be returning to my assignment with Eleanor Channing today. The email back had been short and sweet but the thrust of it was to be careful.

Eleanor's house was noisy when I got there. Yesterday had been an anomaly for Eleanor, to be alone. Today things were back to normal. To be perfectly honest I have no idea what half the people who are around Eleanor do. I know her manager, the cook, the housekeeper, the maids and the bodyguards. Basically I know the people in her life who have easily definable jobs. Then there are the people who just seem to be there to tell her how wonderful she is. Usually I ignore these people. The only reason they speak to me is because as her PA, they believe I can give them more access to Eleanor than they already have.

In the lower foyer, Jorge, one of Eleanor's regular roster of bodyguards that Monique provides, lounged against the wall. Great. That meant we were going out today. Silly me, I thought the fact that your ex-boyfriend had died meant that you'd stay at home and maybe mourn for a minute or two. Obviously not.

"Hope that's strong," Jorge said, looking at the coffee in my hand.

"It always is," I replied.

Jorge was one of the few bodyguards that I could

tolerate. He knew his business and managed to do it discreetly.

"Heard you were there yesterday," Jorge remarked, only looking slightly interested as he drank his own coffee.

"Yeah, I was," I replied carefully.

"Any fallout I should be aware of?" Jorge asked, and this was why he was one of the better bodyguards. Despite the fact the man was huge, like a mountain with tattoos all over him, and biceps which I have on occasion imagined swinging from, he actually had a brain that worked out the possible threats to his charge before they happened. He was also careful in what he did and tried not to trample over too many enthusiastic fans while he did his job.

"She was there when Ryan Hendricks died. You're going to have people who think that she was to blame. Whatever they come up with, whether it is drugs or something else, there are going to be a lot of fans who are going to think it was her fault."

"Do you think it was drugs?" Jorge asked.

"I don't know," I shrugged. "Probably. You know how it is. I didn't think Ryan did drugs but what would I know?"

"Guess you'd better get up to her," Jorge said.

"Have you seen her yet?" I asked.

"Nah, she's still in her room with her therapist. I think the poor shrink ended up having to sleep in her room all night and get woken up on demand."

"Great."

I made my way up the stairs and knocked quietly on the door. Opening it, I found Eleanor still in bed, the therapist sitting in a chair in the corner of the room, looking like she was quietly nodding off to sleep. Eleanor however was awake and just sitting there looking out of the window.

"Miss Channing," I said quietly, trying not to disturb her too much. "Is there anything you need me to get you?"

I didn't really expect anything at this stage. To keep her stunning, impossible for normal people to attain figure,

Eleanor pretty much existed on a no fat, no sugar and no fun diet. This meant coffee, cigarettes, occasional salads and a binge every now and again, followed by a period of self-flagellation with the latest toxin cleansing diet which was making the rounds. During this time, believe me, everyone suffered.

"Do you want to go through your itinerary for the day?" I asked, pulling out my tablet.

"No," sighed Eleanor. "I need you to cancel everything I have today. I'm spending the day at Bliss. I think I need to take care of me today."

I nodded in what I hoped was an understanding way. Considering pretty much every day was all about Eleanor Channing, I didn't get how this would make today any different.

"Are you sure you want to go out in public?" I asked. "Maybe after what happened yesterday it might be good to stay at home rather than spending the day at a spa."

"Bliss is not just a spa," Eleanor said indignantly. "It is a wellness center and I need to heal after the trauma I suffered yesterday. Dr Kennedy said it would be best for me."

Considering Dr Kennedy was probably completely sleep deprived, I wasn't sure how much stock I would put into her advice right about now. That being said, Bliss seemed to be the place to go for everyone. Part spa, part relaxation, all indulgence. The therapists in LA seemed to have locked onto it as the complete cure-all for Hollywood's beautiful and stressed. Luckily it worked on the same priority system as everywhere in LA and Eleanor Channing was close to the top of that priority system.

Eleanor's therapist, grateful that her work seemed to be done, left, but only after reiterating that Eleanor should go alone to Bliss. None of her entourage should be there as Eleanor needed to process yesterday's events and how they affected her life and her future going forward. That meant there were only three of us in the limo heading for Bliss:

Eleanor, Jorge and myself. Jorge, of course, would only be allowed inside the reception area as men were strictly forbidden from the inner sanctum. I, as a woman, was allowed to go in, but there would be no pampering for me. My job was to sit in a corner and be invisible for six hours. I couldn't leave to eat and if I wanted to pee I was out of luck.

Two hours in, I was very discreetly sitting on the edge of the communal bath room. It was based on the old Roman baths concept where women sat in one of the square, in ground baths soaking in some kind of organic concoction. Eleanor had just been relaxing in some milk and honey when there was a sound as the door opened and I looked up into the horrified face of Emily Saunders' PA. Emily Saunders, as in Ryan Hendricks's fiancée, Emily Saunders.

"You slut, how dare you show your face here." Emily shoved her PA to one side and stormed over to Eleanor who was trying desperately to wrap her towel around her wet, and probably sticky from the honey, body.

To Eleanor's credit she did try to make a hasty exit. Nothing like being caught out at being the other woman. Emily Saunders kept yelling at Eleanor using language which, quite frankly, considering she had been portrayed in the media as the sweet innocent darling of tinsel town, quite shocked me.

After sending Jorge a quick help text on my cell, I went to grab hold of Eleanor to get her out, reminding myself to send a very strongly worded note of complaint to the management of Bliss. Something along the lines of making sure staff kept an eye on bookings with relation to current affairs. Unfortunately, as I reached Eleanor, I could see the change in her when Emily made the mistake of calling her a white trailer trash whore. Eleanor Channing was the product of a less than ideal upbringing and she had grown up in some pretty rough places. Despite her delicate look now, I knew from some of the previous stalker incidents with ex-boyfriends, that the woman was able to bring it if necessary. All of a sudden I started being less worried about Eleanor and more worried about how Hollywood princess, Emily Saunders, was going to find herself getting an education on how fighting worked on the streets.

Eleanor grabbed hold of Emily's hair and dove onto her. The two of them ended up on the ground, slapping and scratching. I know when you see fighting on the screen it looks good, but that is because it is choreographed. Fighting in real life, in most cases, looks ridiculous and messy. In this case there was biting and pinching and pulling hair. Eleanor had managed to get on top of Emily. Meanwhile Emily had managed to get hold of Eleanor's arm and left some bite marks on it.

I could hear noise coming from the reception area as voices were raised and hoped that Jorge was able to get in here and help me out. Emily's PA was standing to one side taking video footage as were most of the staff. No one seemed to be at all interested in stopping the cat fight that was going on in front of them.

Hair was flying everywhere as extensions were torn off. Eleanor had managed to scratch Emily's face, but give the girl her due, Emily was putting up a plucky fight. There was no way she could win. Street fighter against princess always ended with the princess being destroyed. Considering she started it, I had trouble feeling sorry for Emily. My mother always told me to never start a fight unless you were sure you could win. Anything else was just plain stupidity.

Sighing heavily, I waded in trying to separate the two women. Neither of them seemed to pay attention to me as I tried to yell out for someone to help me. No one seemed all that interested and kept on filming. In that moment I truly hated the internet.

Trying to pull Eleanor away, I felt arms grab me from behind. Panicking, I flailed backwards and my elbow hit something solid. I heard a quick grunt and then I was flying backwards, thrown to the ground and put in handcuffs, before I knew what happened. Looking up, I saw Detective Griffin with a decidedly annoyed expression on his face and a red mark around his right eye. Oops, that might have been me. Detective Ramos, obviously with a great deal more skill then me, had managed to separate the two fighters and was barking orders about finding the two women some clothes. Oh did I fail to mention that the two of them had lost their towels during the fight. Emily's PA was so much smarter than me. That footage was going to be pure gold.

Looking over, I saw Jorge had finally managed to make it past the reception doors, he must have come in with the cops. He was texting furiously, probably to Eleanor's management. While Ramos was dealing with Emily and Eleanor, and Griffin was dealing with onlookers, Jorge rambled over to me. I had managed to get myself in a sitting position and was contemplating what this little incident meant for my career. I could see myself being blamed by management for this. Not Eleanor's therapist for suggesting the woman leave the house, not Bliss for booking two women who should not be in the same building together, and not Emily and Eleanor for engaging in a schoolyard brawl.

"You okay, cupcake?" Jorge asked in that offhand way of his.

"Do I look okay?" I asked.

"Not really, you look kind of screwed," he said.

"And not in a good way," I replied.

He put a friendly arm around my shoulders. "Don't worry, cupcake, I'm sure this will all be sorted out soon."

"I would suggest you get the hell away from my prisoner," a voice growled at us.

Looking up I could see Detective Griffin and his eyes were narrowed, focused on Jorge's arm around me.

"Sorry, Detective," Jorge said. "Seeya, cupcake," he said to me and then, looking straight at Griffin, he dropped his head and kissed me on the cheek. "Later," he whispered and sauntered off with a cocky grin at Griffin.

Griffin looked back at me and I could see he wasn't amused. Usually I appreciate the humor in Jorge's willingness to not just poke the bear, but slap it up the side of the head with a two by four. Today, not so much. I was the one in handcuffs with a displeased cop that I had, and I cannot emphasize this enough, accidentally hit in the eye with my elbow.

Chapter Seven

After being bundled up in a police car for the second time in two days, I found myself back at the police station. Eleanor and Emily had been transported to hospital. I, on the other hand, was considered a dangerous criminal and was required to sit in the interrogation room for a full hour before Griffin and Ramos walked in again. Griffin had an icepack on his eye which I was willing to bet was just for show. I mean seriously, he'd been hit over an hour ago. The two sat down and I looked at them sourly.

"This is ridiculous, it was an accident. I want my attorney now."

"Okay then," said Griffin, laying the ice pack on the desk between us. "You have requested an attorney so you don't have to speak again until your attorney turns up. Until that moment I am going to talk and I hope you are listening. Since you've been arrested, I have been photographed and I have completed a report regarding the assault I suffered at your hands. You are currently looking at a felony count for assaulting a police officer. If I choose to go ahead and press charges."

"It was an accident." I couldn't believe this was happening.

"It may have been," shrugged Griffin, "or it could have been deliberate. If I press charges we can leave it up to the court to decide. You may be lucky and find a jury who agrees with you, or you may get a jury that isn't happy that a foreigner comes to America and commits felony crimes here. Regardless, your life becomes infinitely more difficult and if you are found guilty and sentenced to jail, even if it is suspended, your green card goes away and you get deported."

"Why would you do that?" I asked, stunned. I was having trouble understanding. I looked desperately at Ramos but her expression was completely blank.

"Alternatively," Griffin said as if I hadn't spoken, "you have another option."

I looked at Griffin and just knew I was not going to like my other option.

"We need to get into the world you are in. We understand that you attend a lot of celebrity events, most of it is not part of your paid work, but you are expected to attend anyway."

I nodded, feeling numb.

"We also understand, it is ostensibly a social gathering for you, despite the fact you are supposed to be working. As a result you are permitted to bring a plus one."

I nodded silently again, knowing that I was not liking where this was going.

"If you would be amenable to me being your plus one for the foreseeable future, I may find you to have acted in the public interest and would be motivated not to press charges."

So there it was, I was going to be blackmailed by the police. They could put any number of pretty words around it but it ended up being the same thing. I had not even had a parking ticket in my life and now I had a felony assault charge hanging over my head. My first instinct was to tell the douchebag, as I was now calling him, to go shove it and get my attorney for me now. Thinking about it though, I knew if I got a record for felony assault I could not only kiss my career goodbye in America. No other country in the world would give me a working visa with that kind of record. Still the idea of working with the evil douchebag after what he was trying to pull was almost more than I could take.

"If I were to agree," I said quietly, "why can't Ramos be my plus one?"

"Because if I'm going to be seen at these things regularly, it's better if I'm your new boyfriend."

"Number one, nobody's going to believe that. You've already been seen as a detective by at least one other staff member. Number two, this is the twenty first century. Nobody's going to blink at me bringing a female plus one."

"Can I please speak to the prisoner alone?" said the douchebag, keeping his eyes on me.

Ramos left the room and the door closed quietly.

"What's your real problem with doing this?" he asked, perfectly calmly, as if destroying my life was nothing to him.

"My real problem," I hissed. I couldn't believe he was being so obtuse. "You know perfectly well I was only trying to break them up before someone got hurt. I didn't even know you were behind me. I got grabbed and I reacted. Now because of that you are threatening to destroy my life. I thought cops were supposed to be the good guys." I could feel the tears pricking my eyes and I blinked furiously to stop them.

He put his hand over mine gently. "We are the good guys, I just need a way in."

I snatched my hand away from him. "Don't touch me," I said with as much venom as I could muster. "I'll do this but only because I don't have a choice. I don't want you touching me at all. You can tell yourself that you're doing the right thing all you want, but underneath it all, you and I both know that the way you are doing this is completely wrong. Once this case is finished, how do I know that you won't still press charges?"

"I give you my word that I won't press charges," Griffin said.

"Strangely enough your honor is not something I am particularly inclined to trust at the moment," I said derisively.

Griffin flinched and it felt good to have got at least one

point on him. "Look," he said angrily. "Ryan Hendricks died of a cardiac arrest."

"If he died of a heart attack, why the hell do you need me?" I asked.

"A week ago Ryan Hendricks had a full medical exam for insurance for a movie he's doing. At that time his heart was perfectly healthy. It doesn't add up. Something happened in the last week that killed him. I need to find out what that was. There's a possibility that there is a new drug on the street that we can't detect. We are getting stonewalled from every side. No one is talking and we don't have enough to force them to talk. This is the only way we have any chance of finding out what happened."

"You could have asked me before threatening to destroy my life," I said.

"Would you have done it?" he asked.

"We won't know now will we?" I said.

"I'm not the bad guy here," Griffin said angrily.

"Sitting on this side of the desk," I said, "yes, you are."

Ramos poked her head in. "Her attorney is here," she said quietly.

"That's okay," said Griffin. "She's free to go."

Ramos handed over my bag.

"I've programmed my number into your cell," Griffin said. "You need to let me know when the next event is."

As I walked past him, he grabbed my arm. "Do you understand what I am telling you?" he said.

"Yes," I replied dully, pulled my arm away and walked towards Reggie.

Seeing my face, Reggie knew not to say anything. Gently he led me out to his car, settled me in the passenger seat and then turned to me.

"Are you okay?" he asked.

I turned to him. "I'm fine," I said, and in one of my not proud moments, I burst into tears.

Dear, sweet Reggie didn't ask anything else. He just wrapped his arms around me and let me sob on his shirt. I was scared and overwhelmed, and right in that moment I just needed someone else to take care of me. In between hiccupping sobs, I told Reggie what had happened.

"I'm taking you to Monique," said Reggie.

"My car is still at Eleanor's," I said.

"Give me the keys and I'll get someone to pick it up and deliver it to your home," he said. "I think the three of us need to sit down and work out what we're going to do."

"I have a deal with the detective," I said. "There's nothing I can do."

"Then we work our way around that. Don't worry, Trudie," Reggie said, with his trademark confident grin. "We won't let anything happen to you."

Chapter Eight

Sitting around Monique's desk, having an impromptu picnic, I started to feel better.

"So how do we get out of this?" I asked, helping myself to some Thai food.

Luckily for me, Monique believes in feeding her people something other than salad. She thinks we need the strength.

"On the surface of it, there is nothing we can do," said Reggie. "According to the letter of the law, you struck a police officer. He now has a black eye so technically he is within his rights to press charges. I've seen cops do it for less. You pull out of this deal and he could just charge you. If you get convicted, you lose your visa and you have a felony conviction on your record. I would of course defend you and I am good." No false modesty there. "But I can't give you a complete guarantee that you would get off. Sometimes things don't go the way they are supposed to."

So, just like I thought. I was screwed.

"Cops use this kind of leverage all the time. They'll give you a lesser charge if you give them information. This is a little bit unusual but it's the same concept."

"My problem," I said, "is that at this stage they have nothing to say that Ryan Hendricks died of anything other than a heart attack. If that's true they could be chasing this for ages. How long am I going to be stuck pretending this guy is my boyfriend?"

"That's where I come in," said Reggie. "We'll go back to the station and organize for this deal to be put in writing with full immunity for you if you cooperate. We will put a time limit on it of a few weeks or as little time as we can get."

Looking at Monique, all I felt was guilt. This was her business and I was royally messing it up.

"I am so sorry, Monique," I said, with my eyes lowered. "As soon as this is done I will quit and you won't be hassled by my problems again."

"Shh, ma petite," she said, her hand cupping my jaw as she raised my eyes to look at hers. "You think this is the worst situation that any of my people have got themselves into? We work in an industry of temptation. Believe me, you are exactly the kind of person I want to keep. In an environment where anything goes, you have remained true to yourself. You are exactly the person that I saw that first day. A sea of calm in the middle of chaos, doing the right thing. You are still doing the right thing. You are just in a bad situation at the moment."

"Thanks, Monique," I said, tears in my eyes again. "I won't let you down, and the second this causes you any problems, I'll quit and deal with the consequences myself."

Once the decision had been made as to what we were doing next, I felt better. I held onto that little piece of happiness when Reggie and I were back in the interrogation room sitting across from Griffin and Ramos. Ramos looked interested in the conversation but I could tell that Griffin was furious. Reggie outlined that I would not be doing anything without an iron clad guarantee that provided me with immunity from the assault charges against me.

"I already told her that I wouldn't press charges if she helped us," Griffin ground out.

"Yes I know you did," said Reggie. "Unfortunately my client's belief in the justice system in this country has taken quite the knock today. She wants to have this agreement signed off by someone other than the man blackmailing her."

Ouch, I thought. That's got to have hurt and I could see from the way Griffin's face tightened that he wasn't too impressed with that comment. I was kind of hoping that Reggie's need to needle Griffin about his tactics weren't going to get me into more trouble.

"I spoke to the District Attorney when you called and we have an agreement," Ramos said. "Detective Griffin will take you into another room to finalize negotiations, Mr Goodman. I will stay in here with Miss Eyre until you're ready to sign it."

Reggie got up and followed Griffin out of the room, leaving me sitting there with Detective Ramos.

"You know, he's not happy about having to do this with you," she said.

"He seems fine with it to me," I replied, not feeling very sympathetic at the moment.

"He's a good guy but we're fighting a losing war at the moment. Between budget cuts and attorneys getting in the way of absolutely everything. In this town, money and prestige talk a lot of the time. We haven't been able to get near Eleanor Channing and Emily Saunders. How the hell are we supposed to do our job?" She sounded frustrated.

"So victimizing the one person in this picture who is completely innocent but just hasn't a way to fight back is the way to go? You're going to try to convince me that that is the right thing to do?" I asked.

"No I'm not," she sighed. "All I'm saying is give him a chance. He doesn't deserve to have you hate him."

"I have no reason not to hate him at the moment," I replied.

"Did you know we have cameras in the parking area?" she said softly. "We saw you lose it in the car with your lawyer."

Great, just another humiliation to add to my already lousy day. I sat there stony faced unwilling to answer.

"I know him and I know it hurt him to see you like that. He's a good man, we're just in an untenable position right now. I'm kind of hoping that you are strong enough to deal with it."

The door opened as Reggie and Griffin walked back in. I searched Griffin's face for any hint of the softness that Ramos was talking about. No, nothing there. When he looked at me all I saw was a granite hard jaw and ice in those green eyes. No nice guy there at all. A piece of paper was placed in front of me. I looked expectantly at Reggie. He didn't seem as happy as I had hoped he would be.

"Trudie, this agreement provides you with immunity from the police assault charge if you agree to provide Detective Jake Griffin with the cover as your boyfriend for a period of three months," Reggie said.

"Months," I spluttered. "But I thought it was only supposed to be a few weeks."

"The charge is a serious one," Griffin interrupted. "It was felt this was a more equitable arrangement."

Definitely no nice guy there. I signed the paperwork reluctantly but I knew I had no options. Once signed I figured Griffin would at least show some sign of his victory but his face gave no indication that he was feeling anything.

As Reggie and I got up to leave, Griffin turned to me. "I want to be invited to everything that you have a plus one invite to," he said.

"I'll call when they happen but it is generally last minute," I said.

"Doesn't matter, this case is a priority now. I'll look forward to your call, sweetheart." He winked at me and sauntered away.

Reggie didn't even look at me once as we made our way to the car. I didn't say a word until we were well clear of the station.

"He called me sweetheart, Reggie," I said through gritted teeth.

"Yes he did," Reggie replied.

"Are you trying not to smile?" I asked, noting that he seemed to be fighting the curl on the corner of his lips.

"A little," said Reggie. "I know you're not happy about

this situation but why don't we chalk it up to a character building exercise."

"You think I need to work on my character?" I asked.

"I'm not going to win, regardless of what I say today am I?" asked Reggie.

"No you're not," I said. "I am in a truly annoyed mood and I don't need reasonable discussion. I need you to say, 'you are right, Trudie, he's an evil lowlife, Trudie, you are by far the better person, Trudie'. If at any time you wish to veer from that script you should just remain silent," I said, feeling a little bit resentful.

"Silence it is then," said Reggie, and so it was all the way back home.

Chapter Nine

I hadn't even made it through my front door when my cell started ringing. It was Eleanor's management again, demanding to know where I was. Once again I had to explain that due to the actions of their client, I had spent most of the day as a guest of LA's finest.

"Never mind that," he interrupted. "We need you to go back to Bliss and find out what was in the products they used for Eleanor today."

"Why do we need to know that?" I asked.

"Eleanor's had a slight reaction to something that was used today. She's still at the hospital but they don't know what it is."

"What kind of reaction?" I asked, hoping my voice showed an appropriate level of interest and concern.

"At this stage it just looks like a mild skin irritation, but if she's allergic to something we need to know what it is. We can't risk her having reactions when she's working."

"It's too late to go tonight," I said, knowing that he expected me to go back to the spa after hours to demand answers from an empty building. "I'll go first thing in the morning."

Dropping my bag on my couch I walked straight into the shower to wash away what had turned out to be a completely lousy day.

The next morning I found myself standing in the reception area of Bliss being eyed off by perky little Cindi, as her badge proudly proclaimed. I could now see why Jorge had not been able to get through to help me yesterday. That door which led to the inner sanctum had an electronic lock. You either needed a security code or access to the little button which was obviously underneath

Cindi's desk. Obviously Cindi had been here yesterday and had seen that I had been led out of here in handcuffs, because she did not seem keen to let me in.

"Hi, look I know things got out of hand yesterday but I am here on behalf of Eleanor Channing. She seems to have had a reaction to some part of the products she had yesterday. I'm just trying to track down what it could have been," I said brightly in a soft non-threatening way, as opposed to a 'we are going to sue this place for all that it is worth' way.

"I'm sorry. I can't help you with that," said Cindi.

I waited but she just looked at me, still with the perky grin. Okay this was obviously going to be a lead the horse to water scenario. Cindi seemed to be incapable of grasping what my problem was.

"Can I please speak to someone who can help me with the situation?" I asked.

"Oh, I'm afraid there is no one else here who can help you," Cindi said brightly, her big smile and excessively white teeth exacerbating the tension headache which was beginning to form behind my right eye.

Either that or Detective Griffin had managed to find a voodoo doll and decided that I needed to feel a bit of his pain.

"Okay Cindi," I said, deciding that bright and friendly was not the way that I was going to play it today. "I need you to get somebody here so I can talk about the reason why Eleanor Channing is still in hospital. A fact that can be related back to this place. If I don't get somebody here right now, who can give me the answers that I want, then I am going to leave. The next time you hear about this situation is going to be from Eleanor Channing's very highly priced legal firm and I will be sure that they include your name in the paperwork. That is Cindi with an 'i' isn't it?"

Cindi looked at me for a second. "If you could please sit down for a minute I will get someone to talk to you," she said.

To her credit that smile did not waver. I was onto her though. Behind that perfectly pleasant face I could tell that she was wishing me at the bottom of a very deep hole. You know what, I could live with that. Being nice and sweet to everybody had got me a job where my life was not my own, at the beck and call of a nutcase with impulse control issues and with a felony charge hanging over my head.

The door opened and a woman came out, perfectly put together and with the serene look that I would expect from someone who worked at Bliss.

"Good morning, I'm Jennifer Saunders. I believe you needed to speak to me."

Oh hell, Saunders. This was Emily's sister. What was the daughter of Henry Saunders doing working in a spa? Deciding to completely ignore the huge elephant in the room I held out my hand.

"Yes Ms Saunders. Thank you so much for agreeing to see me. My name is Trudie Eyre. I need to speak to you about the products used by Eleanor Channing yesterday."

Realization finally reached Jennifer Saunders' eyes and they clouded over. *Yes,* I thought, *that Eleanor Channing. The one who put your sister in a head lock less than twenty-four hours ago.* Keeping my face open and smiling gently, I hoped she could look past my unfortunate associations.

"Ah yes," she recovered beautifully. People are so wrong. Sometimes money can buy class. "Please, call me Jennifer. Let's speak in my office."

Following Jennifer to her office, I wondered what her role at Bliss was. Jennifer Saunders' office was beautiful. Completely impractical with the white suede chairs. I would be able to destroy them in no time at all. The office suited her though, beautiful and calm.

"I didn't realize you worked at Bliss," I said, taking the seat that she indicated with a delicate wave of her hand.

"My husband and I opened Bliss together. My husband

is a strong advocate of the environmental movement and I love the idea of creating beautiful products that are completely natural. Here at Bliss we believe in living in harmony with the environment. As much as is possible we only use what nature provides in our products. A lot of the products we use, we actually grow ourselves on a property on the edge of the city limits," she said, her eyes glowing with enthusiasm.

It was easy to be caught on the wave of her passion.

"I hate to say this," I said, and I truly did. "It seems Miss Channing used a product yesterday while here and it has caused a mild skin irritation."

"Does she have any known allergies?" asked Jennifer, her face creased with concern.

"Not that we know of at this stage," I said, mimicking her concern. "As you can understand though we are very keen to determine if there is a new allergy or intolerance that we have not been previously aware of."

"Of course," she said, turning to her computer and hitting some keys. The printer came to life, spitting out pieces of paper. "I am printing out a list of the products used yesterday by Miss Channing and their ingredients. As her representative I will ask you to sign a non-disclosure agreement for me. I hope you understand."

I signed the piece of paper quite happily.

"Also," she said, "I would like to apologize for the incident that we had here yesterday involving Miss Channing and my sister. The person who was making the bookings was new and had not been aware of the situation between them. We always try to ensure a calm and tranquil space for our clients. I can assure you that a situation like that will not happen again."

Smiling, I took the paperwork. "Thank you very much. I understand that your sister must have been under a great deal of strain yesterday. Maybe her grief got the better of her." I gave her my card. "If there is anything else that you can think of that may have caused the reaction, please call me."

After getting to the hospital I gave the paperwork with the ingredients of the products used on Eleanor to the medical staff. Juggling a coffee, I settled down to wait with Jorge for the next step.

"Glad to see you out of jail," Jorge said.

"Yeah," I said.

"That detective yesterday looked pretty angry when I was talking to you," he mused. I could see the curiosity sparking in his eyes.

There it was. I was going to have to bring Griffin into my world and Jorge had just provided me with an opening.

"Yes, about that," I said. "I've kind of been seeing him lately and he's a bit possessive."

"Wait," said Jorge, looking confused. "You were arrested yesterday by your boyfriend?"

"Doesn't sound good when you put it like that," I said.

"Seemed like a bit of a dick," Jorge said slowly.

"Yeah he did, didn't he?" I replied, matching his tone.

"Doesn't sound to me like he's the kind of guy that deserves you," said Jorge.

That was nice. Jorge and I didn't usually have deep and meaningful conversations but it was good to know that he had my back when it came to my fake, blackmailing boyfriend.

"I don't know how long it's going to last," I said, despite the fact I knew that it was going to last three months and not a second longer.

"Problems already?" he asked knowingly.

"Let's just say he doesn't exactly live up to the advertising," I said sagely. Hell, if I was going to be forced to have the guy as my boyfriend, I was quite happy to trash his reputation while I was at it.

Jorge looked at me with a speculative gleam in his eye. I wasn't really worried. Now Griffin was established as my current, if not future, boyfriend.

One of the nurses who had been working the ward

came over to us.

"Miss Channing has said she wants Trudie to get her ass in there now," she said, with that harried look on her face that I had become used to seeing on the face of anyone who dealt with the woman.

I ducked in the hospital room to find Eleanor strangely subdued.

"Miss Channing, is there anything else you need? I will organize canceling all your appointments for the rest of the day," I said.

"That would be good," she said. "Except the party tonight at Jessica Bailey's house. I'll be attending that. She is such a good friend and I wouldn't want her to think I don't support her."

"Yes, of course," I replied.

Jessica Bailey was a young actress who had managed to get a couple of parts recently that Eleanor had wanted. Going to her party was Eleanor's way of saying that she wasn't scared of the up and comer, that she was perfectly secure in her position. Well, that took care of the rest of the day. Eleanor was so secure in her position that even though the dress code for this party was casual, Eleanor would be spending the rest of the day with stylists, hair and makeup people to ensure that she looked entirely natural for the party tonight.

"I've given the list of the products that were used yesterday on you to the doctors. I believe an immunologist will be in soon to see what they can find out," I said.

"Very well," she replied. "As long as I am ready to leave in time to get ready for tonight."

When the immunologist arrived I ducked out and scrolled through my contacts on my cell looking for my fake boyfriend. There it was, Jake Griffin. I hit the dial button and waited nervously for it to connect.

"I was waiting for your call, Trudie," he answered.

"Hello, Detective Griffin," I stammered. I was a little put off by the fact he knew I was calling. "I'm just letting you know that there is a party tonight at Jessica Bailey's house," I said. "I am not sure if it comes under the terms of our agreement but..."

"What time do I pick you up, Trudie?" he asked smoothly.

"About eight should be fine," I said. "Dress code is pretty casual. The aim for us is to blend into the background."

"I know how to blend in," he said shortly, before disconnecting the phone.

Well that was fun. Can't tell you how much I was looking forward to being his date tonight.

Chapter Ten

By the time Eleanor had been released from hospital and we had gone through the round of stylists and what she should wear, I got home twenty minutes before Griffin was supposed to arrive. I raced into the shower. Lucky for me it wasn't a real date so I was quite happy to let all the regular primping go by the wayside. In my mind, Jake Griffin was only worth the minimum so that is what he got. When the doorbell rang and I hurriedly opened it wearing sweats, I could tell he didn't think much of it.

"Good to see you made the effort," he said.

"I only just got in," I said. "I need five more minutes. Grab yourself a drink if you want."

Hurrying back to my room, I threw on a knee length skirt and a silk top, both conservative, and was out of the room in four minutes and thirty seconds. He looked me over and I could see the word 'boring' flashing through his head.

"I am not going to this thing for fun," I said, grabbing my small clutch. "This is work for me, just like it is for you."

When we got out to the car Griffin opened my door for me. I grudgingly gave him points for effort. I've got to say that it isn't often I get a door opened for me. Once we were headed to the party I wracked my brain for something to say but he started first.

"I heard Eleanor Channing was in hospital for most of the day. I didn't think she got hurt so badly yesterday."

"Oh she didn't. It looks like she had an allergic reaction to one of the products they used at Bliss yesterday before the fireworks started. The products at Bliss are all natural so we needed to get her tested to see if she has developed an allergy to something she is likely to come into contact with on a regular basis."

"Has she?"

"Doesn't look like it. The immunologist went through every product on the list and she didn't have an allergic reaction to any of them."

Silence settled between us again. This felt uncomfortable.

"Should we exchange information about how we met, how we know each other, you know, in case somebody asks?" Griffin said.

"We can but we don't need to go into too much depth. I can pretty much guarantee that no one at this party is going to care about any of that information," I said.

"Why not?" Griffin asked. "Surely you've made friends with this crowd. Don't you go to a lot of these things?"

I sighed. "I go to a lot of these parties, not because I am specifically invited, but because I come with Eleanor Channing. As far as most of the people at these things are concerned, I am part of the furniture and that is the way it should be. I am there to deal with any situation that comes up. I try to stop Eleanor doing anything stupid. I extricate her from difficult situations and I make sure that at the end of the night she is home in bed safe and hasn't done anything to damage the brand," I said.

"Sounds like you don't have much chance for fun," Griffin mused.

"My job is not about fun," I said.

"Then why do it?" Griffin asked. "Are you one of those people who is desperate to have a job in the entertainment industry, willing to do anything until you get your big break?" Griffin's tone was only slightly mocking.

"No," I replied. "I am not interested in becoming an actress. I know I complain about this job but it's what I am good at. I solve problems and I look after people. That is my skill set in life."

The rest of the drive went pretty silently. I really had nothing in common with this man and, to be perfectly honest, I didn't want to have anything in common with him. Once we got to the party, I was surprised to see Jorge at the door and smiled at him as we approached.

"Hi, Jorge," I said. "What are you doing out here?"

"Got here and Eleanor didn't want me. Seems I cramped her style. One of their security guys didn't turn up so I got roped in. This way I'm getting paid twice to be here."

"Smart," I said, still smiling, until I felt an arm go around my waist.

Jorge's face hardened.

"Did you want to introduce us, sweetheart?" Griffin said in my ear loud enough for Jorge to hear.

"This is Jorge. He works security for Eleanor. I've told you about him, honey," I said, patting Griffin on his chest. "This is my boyfriend, Jake," I said sweetly to Jorge.

"The one who arrested you," Jorge said flatly.

"That's the one," I replied.

Jorge looked at Jake scornfully with a slight curl to his lips.

"Go on in. I think Eleanor and her group were upstairs near the balcony," he said, waving us through.

Still holding me close, Griffin leaned down. "That was the guy from yesterday wasn't it?" he asked.

"Yes, that was Jorge." I wondered if you could get a cramp in your face from holding a fake smile too long.

"He didn't seem surprised to see me. Any reason for that?" asked Griffin.

"I might have mentioned today that I had been seeing you," I said as I peered around looking for Eleanor.

"How did you explain me arresting you?"

"I didn't, we just went with the theory that you were a jerk and that the relationship probably wouldn't be lasting long."

Griffin looked surprised. "He seems to have believed that, how are you going to explain us being together the next three months?"

"Never got around to getting rid of you until there was another prospect on the horizon." Griffin frowned but it sounded reasonable to me. People did it all the time.

Griffin lowered his voice. "He could be thinking that you're keeping me around for sex."

"Probably not," I said. "During the conversation I may have intimated that you weren't very good in that area."

"What?" spluttered Griffin.

There really is nothing that upsets a man more than denigrating his bedroom skills.

"Why would you do that?" he said, a little angrily.

"Maybe because I'm really angry that I was having to lie to someone I thought of as a friend and I blame you for that," I hissed.

Griffin grabbed me around the waist and stopped me from stomping away from him.

"Careful, sweetheart," he said. "I may start to believe that you can't wait for this arrangement to be finished."

Looking up into his eyes I measured my words out carefully and softly. "I am counting the hours until I never have to see you again, sweetheart."

I pulled away from him and kept walking towards Eleanor's group. I didn't bother introducing Griffin to anyone. No one would care who he was and I knew that he wanted to maintain a low profile. Eleanor looked him over quickly when she noted that I had arrived, but she didn't seem to register him as the detective who had been at Bliss only the day before. She probably didn't even remember Ramos, even though she had lifted Eleanor bodily off a screaming Emily. Some people were really that self-absorbed.

I took up my normal position on the outskirts of the group. After ordering a drink of soda, I did what I always did and blended into the background. Only this time, Detective Jake Griffin sat beside me and kept watch with me. Of course that only lasted a short amount of time. Watching people get drunk and acting up, even celebrities, gets old really fast. A couple of times, as Eleanor started to become loud and quite abusive, I had to make my way through the crowd and calm her down. Usually I accomplished this task using skills I had learned as a nanny. I found misdirection worked, getting her to focus on someone else or a shiny new toy that someone else had. Sometimes I had bits of gossip that I kept back precisely for these moments. I didn't want to go into what this said about Eleanor or me. During one of these moments I came back and found Griffin had disappeared on me. Good thing he was only my fake boyfriend because I've got to say, if we were a real couple, I would not have been too happy about that. While waiting for him to come back, Crystal sat down beside me.

"What are you doing here?" I asked.

"Networking," she said. "Same as I always do."

"Who's the pretty boy for today?" I asked, straining my neck to look behind her.

Crystal never dated the same guy more than once. Thanks to her dad's company she had a stable of very good looking men that were thrilled to come to these parties with her. Today's selection seemed to be going for hipster trendy with a side of action hero. Not sure if it was working but he seemed to be happy.

"So are you going to tell me why you are with Detective Hottie?" she asked, smiling.

Pulling her aside, I filled her in on the last two days of my life and what they meant for the next three months. After telling her I wondered if I had made a mistake. Those warm chocolate brown eyes of hers were rock hard. Crystal is usually a fun loving person. Underestimating her is something most people do despite her position in her dad's company. I have never made that mistake because I know she has got a temper which can stop traffic and I could see it starting to build. Of course, because that is the way my life goes, Griffin decided to turn up at that precise moment.

Putting an arm around my shoulder he grinned down at me. "Care to introduce us babe."

Crystal's eyes narrowed and she opened her mouth to begin what I am sure was going to be a massive tirade.

"Don't bother with the charade with her, she knows everything. There is no way I could have kept it from her, so there is nothing we can do. She won't say anything but she does think you're a douchebag, just like I do."

Once again using my nanny skills I pointed behind Crystal. "Holy hell, is that Adam Hendricks?"

Crystal spun around. "It is. What would he be doing here?"

I looked behind Adam and groaned. There was Eleanor, holding his hand. She must have got away from the group. From the looks of her mussed up hair, she had decided to use Ryan's brother to help with her grieving. I'd been so caught up with my own drama, I hadn't seen that one coming. I should have though. Adam Hendricks had come to Hollywood with his older brother, but he had just never come close to the same heights that Ryan had. He was always at the parties and events but could never get past being Ryan's younger, not so hot, not so special brother. Looks like that had changed for tonight. Of course the fact he was out partying only a couple of days after his brother died didn't say much for the bond between them. Rumor had it that the Hendricks brothers hadn't been overly fond of each other anyway.

"What the hell is she doing with him?" I asked.

"Why, what's the matter with that?" Griffin asked. I looked at him.

"Really," I said. "You see nothing wrong with the brother and latest lay getting it on only two days after Ryan Hendricks died."

"Interesting way to put it," he said, "but maybe they're just working through their grief together."

"More likely she's getting an invite to the funeral tomorrow," said Crystal.

I turned to Griffin. "The funeral's tomorrow? I thought you guys had the body. Why would you release it so soon?"

"Coroner says heart attack. He's taken all the samples he needs for any further testing we plan on doing. Seems there was pressure to release the body and have this whole sordid mess taken care of."

Griffin did not sound happy. Neither was I. Eleanor at Ryan Hendricks's funeral. With Emily Saunders. That was going to be fun.

"Babe, I want to dance," interjected Crystal's date.

"I'm busy, find something else to do," she snapped. "What?" she said, catching sight of my expression.

"You know I love you," I said, "but sometimes you've got this whole dominatrix thing going on that scares me.

"I'd never aim it at you," she said, smiling.

"I know," I replied, "but what did Sam37 do to deserve that?"

"He's been whining the whole night. He's needy and I don't do needy well," she said.

"Don't I know it," I replied, smiling.

"I'm sorry," said Griffin, "but I think I missed something. Who is Sam37?"

"That's her doing," said Crystal, pointing at me.

"Crystal dates a lot of men from her dad's casting agency and it just got too hard to keep up with all the names," I said. "Our friend, Edwin, and I started calling them all Sam. We give them numbers to differentiate them. Tonight's effort is Sam37."

"Are you judging me, Detective?" Crystal said sweetly. "I hope not because you're blackmailing my friend. I really don't think you're in a strong enough moral position to judge me." With that, she kissed me on the cheek, whispered, "call me when you get home," and walked off.

"She goes for the balls doesn't she?" said Griffin, frowning as he watched Crystal walk away.

"She's way tougher than she looks. Most people don't

really see it. I've seen her rip into men who were standing over her and she can back it up."

"She's George Bronstein's daughter isn't she?"

"Have you been researching us?" I asked.

"Seemed a good idea," he shrugged.

"In answer to your question, yes, she is George Bronstein's daughter but she had an interesting childhood which culminated at nineteen with her getting involved with a bikie. I'm not talking an accountant who rode motorcycles on the weekend either. I'm talking a hide your daughters, lock up the silverware, and why is the sheriff riding out of town, kind of bikie. She got away from that kind of life pretty soon after that, but not before she absorbed the attitude and some pretty interesting life skills."

"You sound like you admire her," Griffin said.

"I do," I said. "She had a pretty lousy childhood being used as a cash cow by her mother and yet she's come through it okay. She also adores her father and is very protective of him and her friends, and that is why she hates your guts."

"Why did you have to tell her the truth about our arrangement?"

"Lying to her was never going to happen. The people I know best in LA are Reggie, Monique, Crystal and my friend, Edwin. I could not get away with lying to them. They know me too well and would have suspected something and got in the middle of it anyway. This way they are in the know but you can be sure they won't say anything to anyone. It's the best I can do," I said.

"Okay," Griffin said. "I'll trust your judgment on this one."

"You are just full of the sweet talk," I said sarcastically.

Looking as if he was desperate to change the topic, Griffin looked around. "Is it always like this?"

"What, the celebrity scene?"

"Yes I was expecting it to be more, I don't know," he

said, waving his hand in the air.

"More exciting," I filled in. "More interesting, less desperate alcohol and drug fueled hookups."

"Yeah I guess so."

"They're people," I said. "Just a bit amplified.

I could see that Eleanor was getting ready to leave and went over to her.

"Are you okay?" I asked her. Her eyes were overly bright and I was a little concerned that she might not have just been indulging in alcohol tonight. I lowered my voice. "Were you safe with Adam?"

"You always worry about me don't you?" she said, patting her hand against my cheek.

"Of course I do," I said.

"I think you're the only person I can really depend on."

Oh no, please don't let her start crying on me. When Eleanor gets drunk she gets maudlin. The last time she got drunk, she cried over me about how I was her only true friend. The next morning she screamed at me for being the moron who couldn't get her coffee right. You learn to take the good with the bad.

"I'm going to the funeral tomorrow," she whispered. "Adam said Ryan would want me there. He said I was the one Ryan really loved."

I wondered if that was before or after Adam got her naked. Not my problem. I just had to get her into the car and away from here before she decided to kick on through the night and things really got out of control. I put my arm around her waist and indicated to her entourage that they were finished for the night. Grumbling ensued and I quirked my eyebrow at them. Hey look, it worked. Maybe I had learned something good from Griffin. Speaking of which, the detective was beside me.

"Is there something you need me to do?" he asked as Eleanor listed against my side.

"Just clear the way for us and try to make sure no one is taping this." I swear the person who thought it was a good idea to put cameras on phones is an idiot and every day I hate them just that little bit more. These days everyone thinks they can be a photojournalist and are just waiting for the shot that is going to make them millions. At that moment Jorge materialized on the other side of Eleanor and took some of the weight from me. I smiled at him gratefully and he winked at me.

"I'll get her home safe," he said as I pushed her into the back of the limo.

"Thanks, Jorge," I said as he got in.

"She's going to the funeral tomorrow," I let him know.

"That's not good," Jorge said, frowning.

"Tell me about it," I said. "I'll contact her manager and tell him what's going on. Maybe he can talk her out of it."

"Hope so," said Jorge, getting into the car while throwing a scowl in Griffin's direction.

"He really doesn't like me does he?" said Griffin as the car drove off.

"Doesn't look like it," I said.

"You two dated?" Griffin asked.

"No, just worked together," I said.

As we settled in the car I remembered to ask. "Where did you disappear to tonight?"

"Just went looking to find anything that might be interesting," he said.

"Did you find what you were looking for?" I asked.

"Not really," he replied. "I saw some things that might interest the drug squad. Found a lot of people in various stages of undress, but other than that it seemed kind of tame."

"Have you given any thought to the fact that there might not be a new drug out there, that it just may be one of those things?" I asked.

"Look, that is always a possibility," Griffin said. "I've just got this gut feeling that Ryan Hendricks didn't die from natural causes. I really think this is the best way to find out what actually killed him."

"Okay," I said.

"Just okay," he said. "No 'you're a blackmailing jerk who is trying to ruin my life'."

"Oh you are that, but I have to agree with you. I think there is something strange going on here. Ryan Hendricks was a health nut and he treated his body like a temple. He trained hard, didn't do drugs or smoke. I don't even think he drank alcohol. He was always spouting that organic was the way to go. He seemed to be determined to live forever."

"See this is why I need you," Griffin said. "This kind of information is something that nobody else has been telling us."

I looked at him as he drove. He was a strong-looking man, his hands on the steering wheel controlled the truck with assuredness. He looked good tonight. I'd been so mad at him, I hadn't even noticed but he'd made an effort. He'd also made an effort with me. I hadn't been in the mood to appreciate that he'd been polite with me and opened doors for me.

Quietly I said, "Look I understand why we are doing this. You need to know that threatening me the way you did scared me a lot. I'm in a place here where I'm happy. I have people around me who I care about a lot. You threatened to rip me away from that. I know my job may not seem important to you but I'm proud of what I do. I'm having trouble getting past what you did."

By this stage we'd pulled into the parking area of my apartment complex.

Griffin turned around and looked at me. "I understand and I am sorry that what I did scared you," he said.

He got out of the truck and came around and opened the door for me. Silently he walked me to the door of my apartment.

As I unlocked the door he said, "I'll be at the funeral tomorrow in my official capacity so I won't be able to take you."

"That's okay," I said. "I'll be going with Eleanor anyway. Just remember, if there is a fight and I'm trying to pull her off, please just leave me be, or tell me before you grab me. I can't afford another assault charge."

He smiled as I ducked inside and closed the door. Leaning against it, I realized that I was no longer afraid of Detective Griffin, but that smile and the way it made my stomach flip. That smile was dangerous.

Chapter Eleven

The next morning the first thing I did was to contact Eleanor's management and try to put forward my case, in the strongest form possible, that Eleanor attending Ryan Hendricks's funeral was a disaster waiting to happen. As usual though, Eleanor had made her decision and there was nothing that anyone could do or say that would change her mind. That was why I was standing at the church in black pants and flat shoes, because if things went to hell, I was prepared for it. Eleanor, of course, was dressed in a wildly inappropriate deep red dress which had a thigh split leaving very little to the imagination.

"It was Ryan's favorite dress on me," she would impart in a breathy whisper to anyone who looked at her strangely. Today, Eleanor's manager and publicist had also chosen to accompany her, in the hopes of averting a repeat of the Bliss incident. In my opinion, considering the dress she was wearing, I wasn't holding my breath. Adam Hendricks was dressed in a black suit, his face appropriately somber. He was at the front of the church and appeared to be consoling Emily Saunders, who was leaning heavily on her sister, Jennifer. Jennifer looked drawn and seemed to be holding up Emily. The tears streaming down Emily's face seemed to have a devastating effect on her sister and I could see Jennifer was whispering into her ear throughout the service.

Adam Hendricks gave a eulogy which leaned a little too heavily on how much he had sacrificed so that his brother could shine. A little self-serving for my tastes but in a town where even a funeral was considered a networking event, it was pretty much standard. Keeping Eleanor and Emily apart at the funeral was a lot easier than I thought it was going to be and everyone made their way to Ryan Hendricks's house for the wake. Of course, this was not the house he had died in. No, that would have been tacky. This was Ryan's main house, the one used by tourist buses to point out the glamorous lives that actors led. Adam was at the door greeting people as they came in. It seemed he was running the show as Emily was nowhere to be seen.

"How are you holding up, Elly?" he asked solicitously, as he hugged Eleanor for just a few moments too long to be entirely appropriate.

"I'm trying to be strong," she sniffed delicately, "but it's so hard."

She was also trying very hard not to slap him. Calling Eleanor Channing, Elly, was considered a mortal sin right up there with providing her with the wrong coffee.

"I know." Adam shook his head sorrowfully. "I still keep expecting him to walk through the door and tell me it was all simply a hoax."

For a second I stopped. Could it have been? I'd heard worse, but then I stopped and realized, no, it wasn't possible for it to be a hoax. I was there. There was no way that Ryan Hendricks was still alive. I hadn't been that freaked out that day. Once I had managed to ensure that Eleanor was sequestered in a corner with her manager and publicist, I decided to look around and see what information I could glean from the people attending the wake.

The best part of my job is that I can wander around a party and no one realizes that I'm even there. Some would call it slightly unethical. I just call it being aware of my environment. Wallflowers get the best information and sometimes that information could help me do my job. Today though, most of the gossip was centered on the fact that Ryan had been with Eleanor when he died. Cheating on your fiancée was not necessarily considered to be a great sin. Dying while with the other woman was considered to be a bit of a social faux pas.

"You look as bored as I am," said Jennifer Saunders as she sidled up to me.

"I'm here for work," I said.

"I know the feeling," she replied.

I looked at her strangely.

"Ryan was Emily's fiancée," she said as if in explanation. "I'm here as support for her."

"Oh, of course," I said. "I would have thought your parents would be here too."

"No, Mom and Dad weren't too keen on Ryan. They thought he had a bit of a wild reputation and they didn't really think he was the right man for Emily."

That was news. The media had been playing up the whole blissful love story angle. I had just naturally assumed the whole family was behind the marriage. I could understand their concern though. Ryan was a bit of a wild man when it came to women. There were movie sets where he had pretty much gone through the entire female cast and some of the crew by the end of the shoot. If I had a daughter, I would slap her in a chastity belt before I let her anywhere near Ryan Hendricks.

"How's she holding up?" I asked.

"Pretty devastated," Jennifer sighed. "I think she still can't believe it. I was hoping that if she threw herself into her work that might help."

I drew a blank. I honestly didn't know what work Emily Saunders did. I'd always thought she was some vacuous socialite who lived off her trust fund but then look at Jennifer. I probably assumed the same about her as well. I would never have guessed in a million years that she had opened up a spa or wellness center. Maybe I should look a little closer at my preconceptions. Maybe I'd been working too long with these people and was getting bitter. I mean look at Crystal. Before I became friends with her I would have lumped her into the exact same category as Emily and Jennifer. I looked at Jennifer with new found respect.

"Anyway," she said, "I should get going. Adam has told me he'll take care of Emily and I left my husband at home today. Josh has a tendency to get so involved in his work that he forgets basic things, like eating and showering."

I smiled. That was nice and normal.

She gripped my hand. "Thank you, it was nice talking to you."

"It was good seeing you too," I said.

After Jennifer left I found myself wandering through the house again. Walking down one of the hallways, I saw a door that looked interesting and opened it. I froze. In that moment I did not know where to look because I saw Emily Saunders backed up against the wall, her legs wrapped around the hips of Adam Hendricks. Her head was arched back and his pants were around his ankles. Sadly enough this was not a new situation for me. My mother always said that I have a curiosity gene that leads me to trouble, and a deficiency in me that makes me follow that curiosity. In this town it meant that I had come across quite a few people in this position before. I heard people coming down the hallway and I panicked. Trying to close the door as quietly as possible, I went to flee before getting caught when a strong arm grabbed me around the waist. Before I knew it I was pinned against the hallway wall and somebody's mouth was fastened to mine. My first instinct was to struggle but the lips left my mouth and I heard Griffin whisper.

"It's me. Just go with it."

He returned to my lips and despite my shock I started to realize that the man may be a jerk, but he could kiss. I was feeling this kiss right down to my toes. Part of me put that down to my very long dry spell since the last time that a man kissed me. Griffin's hands stroked up and down my side and then settled on my hips. His lips left mine again and I tried to chase them. He chuckled darkly as he started placing butterfly kisses down my neck. I'm not proud of this fact, but in that moment, if he had pulled me into a dark room, I would have done whatever he asked of me. Once again, I am putting that moment of insanity down to my long dry spell. The people in the hallway passed by and when they were out of sight Griffin lifted his head.

"They're gone," he said softly.

"What," I said, still dazed and looking at that beautiful mouth which had just lit some major fires in me.

"Sweetheart," he said, "you gotta stop looking at me like that or I'm not going to be responsible for what happens next."

That snapped me out of it. The last thing I needed was to complicate this situation even more than it already was. I wrenched myself away and slapped a hand on his chest.

"What the hell was that for?" I asked indignantly.

"That was to stop you from getting caught for the snooping you were doing. Didn't your mother ever tell you it was rude to go through people's houses, especially during a wake," he said.

"My mom kind of gave up on my manners when she found out how curious I was and that I never listened," I said.

"I bet you were a stubborn one," he chuckled again.

Hearing the door opening behind us, Griffin slammed me back up against the wall. This time there was no foreplay and no coaxing. He hooked my leg over his hip and slammed his mouth down on mine. Using his tongue against the seam of my mouth, I relented and he swooped in as if determined to taste every part of me.

"Room's free if you want it dude," I heard Adam Hendricks say.

Next thing I knew, my other leg was hooked up and I was carried into the room, the door was shut and I was pressed against it. I felt fingers at the buttons of my top and cold reason came rushing back in. I pushed back against his chest.

"Stop," I gasped. "What are you doing?"

"Just trying not to get caught this time," said Griffin,

breathing heavily.

"What are you doing here?" I asked, trying really hard not to notice or acknowledge that despite everything else, there was a part of him that was really enjoying this moment.

"I came to see if there was anything I could pick up during the memorial service."

"I thought it was a funeral."

"There wasn't a body," he said.

"Why wasn't there a body?" I asked.

"At the last moment I presented information to the lieutenant and he believes that there may be reason to view this as a homicide. The coroner kept hold of the body for more tests."

"But if there's no funeral," I said, "why all this? They could have just canceled and waited for the body to be available."

"Looks like the show had to go on," Griffin shrugged.

I'd got momentarily distracted. That movement reminded me that I was currently pinned to the door with my legs wrapped around the lean hips of a man that I was really not very fond of.

"Are you planning on letting me down?" I asked as I tried to wriggle myself away from him.

I looked up and got caught by the way his eyes darkened. I flushed as I realized what I was doing and the response that I was inciting in him. Okay, bad move. I stopped the wiggling and waited for the under pressure detective to calm himself down, although by the feel of him it was going to take a lot of calming. I dropped my legs and he stepped away. I tried desperately to stop my hands from shaking as I discovered that a couple of buttons had managed to come undone in our little effort. Although from the way he was looking at me they might not have come undone by themselves.

"So what was that all about?" I said, while tucking the ends of my shirt back into my very sensible pants.

"I needed to keep my face hidden," he said. "I'm not supposed to be here."

Great. He had virtually guaranteed I would not be sleeping tonight from frustration as I replayed those kisses in my mind, and from his perspective I was performing the same function as a balaclava. Wonderful.

"So making it seem like I was the type of person to make out at a wake seemed like a good idea," I said, cringing as I realized I had been making out at a wake.

"No, just an added bonus," he said, smirking.

Yeah, that was why I hated this guy.

"Anyway," he said. "Considering the people who saw you were the brother and fiancée of the deceased and they had just been having sex in this room, I don't think they are able to hold the high ground on this one."

I stopped. "I've got to say, I didn't see that one coming. I thought she was a lot more innocent than that." I shrugged. "Of course innocent in this town is relative, it just means you haven't released a sex tape yet."

Griffin made some kind of noise as if he was choking.

"Are you okay?" I asked, wondering why I was concerned.

"Fine, fine," he said, clearing his throat. "Just not expecting you to start talking about sex tapes."

I raised an eyebrow at him. "Just a general comment. Not planning on starting a whole discussion on it. So if you don't need me to act as a human Richard Nixon mask I assume I'm fine to leave," I said.

I needed to go home. I also needed to wipe the last ten minutes from my memory and I had a feeling that was going to take a bit of time. I wondered if cold showers really worked. No guy had ever managed to get me this worked up over just a kiss before, so I was in uncharted territory.

Opening the door, Griffin peeked out. "The coast is clear, you should be okay now."

Slipping past him I'd almost made it out when a hand

grabbed my elbow.

"I'll be seeing you later, sweetheart," he said huskily, and then let me go and headed in the opposite direction.

I shivered involuntarily. I was so in over my head with this one, I couldn't even see where the problem began. Heading downstairs, I heard loud voices with Eleanor's voice rising over the top of them. I raced down the stairs to find Eleanor and Emily at it again. Luckily, this time security had got between them in the form of the biggest man I had ever seen. He even made Jorge look normal. Actually he looked kind of bored standing between two tiny women, like he knew he had a job to do but he couldn't believe it had come to this. Adam Hendricks had his arms around Emily Saunders as she screamed obscenities at Eleanor. Once again, I've got to say that the woman was surprising me. The creativity behind some of those insults was more than I thought she was capable of. Of course all the insults flying followed the same home wrecking slut, no talent whore, kind of topic, but they were creative. Slipping behind Eleanor, I stood next to the publicist and leaned over.

"What's happening this time?" I asked.

"What the hell am I supposed to do about this?" the woman snarled.

When the publicist is stumped, you know the situation is bad. One thing I have learned about these people is that they are eternally optimistic. No matter how bad a situation, they are able to spin the press in a positive way. When your publicist gives up, you know you are in trouble. Eleanor's manager was trying to pull her away and seemed to be earning his hefty fees for once. After the last time I was not getting involved in this situation. I knew that Griffin was prowling around the building somewhere and I already owed the guy three months. There was no way, especially after that scene earlier, that I was going to risk extending my period of servitude.

Eventually we managed to get Eleanor into the limo

and the manager, her publicist and I just looked at each other with the same expressions our parents must have used when we messed up badly.

"Rehab," the publicist blurted out.

The manager and I looked at her. Eleanor ignored her completely and continued to drink champagne out of a bottle. Inwardly I chuckled. This was going to be good.

"Exactly where do you think you are going with that thought?" I asked. "Or are we just brainstorming and throwing words out to see what works."

"Hear me out," she said. "Eleanor has gone through a traumatic situation. Ryan died on her just as he realized he had made a terrible mistake. That she was his one true love. He called her to beg her to give him another chance. She went to see him and they talked all night about their dreams for a future together and how they could deal with the situation without hurting Emily."

This woman was wasted in public relations, she should be writing screenplays, very fictional screenplays.

"She witnessed the tragic death of her one true love."

She was warming up to the story, I could see. Real life had no part in this and I could see the manager was getting hooked in as well.

"The last two days have been terrible for her, so she is exhausted and needs time to heal. We put her in one of those rehab places for a few days so she can deal with her grief."

"Not trying to rain on your parade," I said, indicating the woman who was still drinking out of the champagne bottle as we discussed her impending, and I'm guessing, involuntary, entry into rehab. "Is she actually going to have to take part in a detox program? If she is, I'm not liking your chances."

"Oh, of course not. I know just the place for her. It'll be more of a holiday for her. She can have everything she wants, she'll just be away from temptation."

"The temptation to smash her fist in Emily Saunders'

face," I said.

"Yes that would be it." The publicist was nodding enthusiastically, obviously hoping that the rest of us could also see her vision.

"That is a perfect idea," the manager said, beaming.

The self-congratulatory smiles were interrupted by a soft snore coming from the other side of the limo. Eleanor Channing had fallen asleep while we had been discussing her future, her hand still firmly wrapped around the neck of that champagne bottle.

Chapter Twelve

The next morning I was woken up by my cell phone. I couldn't believe it. After bundling Eleanor up and getting her settled into the Happy Valley Relaxation Center, I had been sure that I was about to get my first decent sleep. For a full week Eleanor Channing was no longer my problem. She was the problem of the insanely happy people at the relaxation center. Considering how cheerful those people had been when we rolled up at two in the morning with a decidedly annoyed Eleanor Channing, there was no way there weren't any happy pills in that place. There was a part of me that really wanted to ignore the phone but it kept on going. Knowing my luck, Eleanor had staged a jail break from the center and I was going to have to hunt her down, fugitive style. I wallowed in that fantasy for a while, but as with all my fantasies at the moment, Jake Griffin turned up and made the whole thing feel way hotter. Grabbing the phone I put it to my ear.

"Hello," I croaked.

"Good morning, sweetheart," Griffin's voice came through and every nerve ending in my body went on high alert.

"Why are you torturing me, Griffin?" I groaned. "What did I ever do to you?"

"You gave me a black eye, sweetheart," he said.

"And I am in hell because of that. Do you really need to add a paper cut with lemon juice to my already over the top punishment?" I asked.

Griffin chuckled. What that deep voice did to me. I didn't know how I was going to last for three months without jumping on him and wrapping my legs around him and, oh yeah, I already did that. I was in so much trouble.

"Just wondering when we are going to have our next date," he murmured.

"Not for a week," I relished telling him.

"Why not?" he asked. "I thought Eleanor Channing was much more social than that."

"Oh she is," I assured him. "But as of last night, or rather very early this morning, Eleanor Channing checked herself into a relaxation center, to deal with the trauma of losing the love of her life so tragically."

"You are kidding me aren't you?" Griffin said.

"Nope," I answered. "You'll be able to read all about it on her website and social media, where she'll assure her fans that she is strong but just needs some time to heal."

"Okay," Griffin said. "You still have access, maybe you can just go yourself."

"Oh, honey." See I can do sarcasm as well. "Without Eleanor Channing I am nobody. None of these people are my friends, none of them even know my name. I may be able to get you into a book club but that is the extent of my social life."

"What about your friend, Crystal? I'm sure she'd be able to help."

"Crystal doesn't like you very much," I said. "I really don't see her helping you at all. Maybe you should do some actual police work for the next week. Who knows? You may be able to solve this case without me."

I know, I was being a bitch and normally I try very hard not to be a bitch. I don't like women who think being a bitch means being strong, but Jake Griffin put me on edge. Last night had made me think about things I hadn't thought about in a long time. Things which weren't possible, so if being a bitch made sure they never happened again, then that was what I was going to have to do. There was silence for a second.

"I'll do that," he said quietly.

I was about to apologize. I don't like making people feel bad. It's really not who I am.

"I don't think you're a nobody," he said and hung up.

Great, now I really felt lousy. The phone rang again.

"Look, I'm really sorry," I said.

"Why didn't you tell me?"

I stopped and tried to change gears. "Jennifer, is that you?" I asked.

"Why didn't you tell me?" she repeated.

"Tell you what?" I asked.

"I just got paperwork from Eleanor Channing's attorneys about the skin reaction she had. She's suing me."

Oh hell. What kind of a boneheaded move was Eleanor making this time?

"Look, Jennifer, I knew nothing about this. I'm really sorry but there is nothing I can do about it."

"Could you come out and talk to me?" she asked. "I just need to get a bit of an idea about what is going on and why she is doing this."

"Jennifer, I really don't think that is appropriate," I said. "I still work for Eleanor and if she is suing you I can't talk about it."

"I just need someone to talk to," she sniffed.

Oh no, she was crying. I can't handle people who cry. I have a highly developed empathetic nature. On one hand it means that I am as far away from a psychopath as you can possibly get. On the other it means that when someone is upset I am just as likely to start bawling as they are.

"I'll come to Bliss as soon as I can," I said, knowing I was going to regret this.

"I'm not at Bliss today," she said with a hitch in her voice. "I'm at home, can you come out here?"

I agreed and took down the details. Once I was off my phone, I threw off the covers. Getting dressed, I cursed the part of me that wanted to take care of everyone. Monique saw it as a plus. All I saw was the number of times it had got me into trouble. Pulling on my jeans and trainers, I figured I wasn't needing to impress anyone today.

Driving up to Jennifer's property, I was taken aback by how beautiful it was. After six months in LA, I was getting used to the crush of people in the city and the unrelenting development, but I had grown up in country Australia. I'd lived in a tiny town where everyone knew everyone else. Most importantly, I was used to heaps of space and bushland. I love the frenetic pace of my life in LA but every now and again I miss the quiet that I had in Australia. This place reminded me of why I missed it. LA surprises you like that sometimes.

After being buzzed through the gate, I didn't have time to knock on the door before Jennifer Saunders wrenched it open, threw her arms around me and started sobbing. I awkwardly patted her on the back. Seeing her husband nearby, I tried to indicate with my head that he should be here dealing with this. He just seemed to duck his head and scurry away. I groaned inwardly. I know there are some men in touch with their feelings who can deal with female emotion, but why have I never met them?

"Why is she trying to ruin me?" she asked.

I shrugged my shoulders. I didn't have an answer.

"Did you want to go for a walk?" I asked.

Truth be told, I badly wanted to have a look at this place. I could not believe there was a block this large so near to the bustle of Hollywood.

Jennifer hooked her arm into mine. I have to say it felt a little too familiar considering we just barely knew each other and she had asked me here because my boss was suing her. I wasn't sure what had suddenly made us best friends but obviously she needed someone and I was all that was available. That struck me as being really sad. Meanwhile Jennifer had morphed into a tourist guide.

"We grow a lot of our own ingredients for our products at Bliss," she said as we walked through the grounds.

I was amazed. Most celebrity houses that I had seen in LA had the grounds filled with big houses, pools and entertaining areas. This place had vegetables, fruit and in a back corner I could even see a bee hive nestled against a fence which seemed to back on to a national park.

"You have a bee hive?" I asked excitedly.

"Yes, Josh is so interested in the way the environment works as a whole. He thinks it's important that we contribute to all aspects of the ecosystem," Jennifer said. "He is very passionate about it."

I looked at her sharply. I hadn't missed the note of sadness in her voice.

"He spends all his time working on our products at Bliss and with the new organic cleansing diet line that we are promoting at the moment, our lives are just so hectic. We live in the same house but we hardly get to see each other."

I nodded silently. I've learned when people are talking and are highly strung emotionally, adding your opinion does not help the situation. The best thing to do is let them talk themselves out. I didn't know what had brought this on but I could guess that getting the paperwork from Eleanor's lawyers had pushed this woman to her limit. She was trying to hold her life together as well as support her sister in her time of need, and now she was being sued. A cynical part of me had the feeling that daddy was going to be brought in to deal with this issue, or maybe that was what Eleanor wanted. She had already put herself on the wrong side of Henry Saunders by fooling around with his daughter's fiancée and then having public fights with his daughter. Usually that would be seen as making a stupid career move. Maybe this was Eleanor's way of getting a bit of leverage over the studio head. I wouldn't put it past her. Eleanor could be ruthless when she wanted something. So it looked like because of her power play I now had an emotionally distraught woman to deal with. I led her to a rock wall and sat her down.

"Why did you ask me to come here?" I asked her.

"I don't know," Jennifer said. "You were just nice to

me. People are sometimes so rude and mean but you were nice. You didn't expect anything from me, you just talked to me. I get so many people who just want to get to know me because of my father or my sister. I'm not like them. I just want to live my life. I just felt like I could talk to you. I know you can't do anything about the lawsuit. I just needed to talk to someone."

"That's okay," I said soothingly, even though my discomfort level was heading higher. "If you need to talk, just do it. I'll listen."

She seemed to gather herself at that point. "No, I'm sorry," she said, standing up quickly. "I should never have presumed to call you here. It wasn't fair of me to do that. I was just taken a bit by surprise." Quietly she turned to me. "She's doing it because of Emily and Ryan isn't she?"

"I don't know," I said honestly, although that was my theory, and from the look of it she was pretty sure of it too.

Saying my goodbyes to Jennifer I felt like going to the relaxation center and kicking Eleanor Channing. Some people in this world deserve to be kicked and Eleanor was currently at the top of my list.

Chapter Thirteen

Going back to my apartment, I realized that I now had a whole week of freedom. I hadn't had any time off in four months, so I was going to need a plan to deal with this unexpected turn of events. I was excited. Maybe I could go away for a couple of days. I was still getting paid by Eleanor, which I refused to feel guilty about. I had only taken two steps into my apartment when there was a knocking at the door. I wrenched it open and noted that I always seemed to answer my door in a bad mood. That couldn't be good. Crystal and Edwin were there and they walked past me and sat down before I even had a chance to invite them in.

"I've spoken to Edwin," Crystal said imperiously, "and we have decided that the only way to get you out of your problem with Detective Hottie is to find out how Ryan died ourselves."

I was quiet for a second. I had several issues with that statement. Starting at the top, Edwin and Crystal didn't decide. Crystal told Edwin what was going to happen and Edwin just agreed. Though he tried to hide it, Edwin was nuts about Crystal and would find his way to the moon if she asked it of him. Of course, Crystal was completely oblivious and Edwin was not willing to risk never seeing her again by making a move, so the three of us continued in a painful dance. Secondly, I hadn't realized that Detective Griffin was now officially known as Detective Hottie. Obviously my introduction the other night had not changed her mind on that score. And lastly, Crystal's belief that we could solve a death, that the police were not even sure yet whether it was a homicide, kind of beggared belief. It did however sound good that she believed that we were capable of doing such a thing. At this point Crystal and Edwin were looking at me, obviously expecting my wholehearted approval of this plan.

"Uh, do you really think that is a good idea? Considering how much trouble I am already in with the LAPD. I have an assault on a police officer charge hanging over my head remember. Do you think I want to go sticking my nose in this mess?"

"You've got the time now," said Crystal.

Obviously she would know about Eleanor being away for a week. Crystal always knows everything. The woman has a network of intelligence that would put some countries to shame.

"I don't think the fact I have a week without work should be the deciding factor in this situation," I said.

Edwin put his hand over mine. "It isn't," he said. "We're just not willing to lose you." I started tearing up but he continued. "This detective is threatening to send you home. That isn't acceptable to us."

Okay I was really going to cry now. In Edwin and Crystal, I had found true friends, evidenced by the fact they were willing to hunt down a possible murderer to keep me close.

"Thank you," my voice croaked. "I appreciate the idea but do we have an actual plan?"

"Yes," said Crystal, standing up, brushing down her skirt. "We're going back to the place where Ryan died."

Not the plan I was thinking of. "Wouldn't the police still have control of that house?" I asked.

"No," she said. "They've finished their investigation there."

"Any plans on how we are going to get in or do you have the skills to break in?" I asked.

Crystal seemed affronted that I would even ask the question. "Oh I could get us in if I wanted to," she said proudly

Of course she could.

"But in this case I don't need to. Adam Hendricks gave me the key."

"Just as a question, why did Adam Hendricks give you the key to his brother's house?" I asked.

Crystal looked at me as if I was an idiot. Of course. Adam Hendricks would give her anything she wanted. She was the gateway to one of the biggest casting agents in Hollywood. For an actor who hadn't quite made it yet, she was the key to the Promised Land. The man would probably give her the house if she wanted it. Luckily we only needed it for a couple of hours.

Pulling up to Ryan Hendricks's house felt like deja vu. There was a small part of me that didn't want to go inside. Edwin whistled low in his throat.

"Nice place," he said. "Very private."

"It needed to be," I said. "This is his second house for when he wanted to do something that wasn't quite right for public consumption."

"So what was he into?" asked Edwin as we went up the stairs.

"Actually," I said, "if you didn't take into account that he slept with anyone in a skirt, he wasn't too bad. He took his craft seriously, didn't do drugs, and didn't drink much at all."

"He used to be great on set," Crystal chimed in. "He was always at work on time, we never had any problems with complaints from producers or directors, unless there was a wife or girlfriend involved."

Looking through the house, we could see where the police had already been. As I feared, there was nothing that we could find that gave any indication of why a healthy man in the prime of his life had succumbed to a heart attack. In the kitchen we had a look around and I opened the massive fridge. In it there were boxes of organic fruit and vegetables and bottles of juice.

"How much of this stuff did he need?" I asked.

Edwin peered over my shoulder. "Looks like he was on

that cleansing diet that a lot of celebrities are using to detox their systems," he said.

"How long is it supposed to last?" I asked.

"About five days," Edwin replied.

"There is a lot more than five days' worth here," I said.

"Some people are on it longer if they're trying to lose weight," Edwin said. "Not exactly how you're supposed to do it, but it's one way to go."

"Ryan Hendricks did not need to lose weight," I said. "The man was in amazing shape."

"Actually," Crystal interrupted, "he would have been trying to lose weight."

"Why?" I asked.

"New movie is making the rounds at the moment. Don't have many details but the lead role has a guy who is really thin, as in sick thin. I know Ryan was interested. This role is Oscar material and I think he was getting tired of playing the lead in romantic comedies and action movies. This was his chance to show that he could really act. Word is that Ryan had decided to try to go into the audition as thin as possible to show he could do it."

Shutting the refrigerator door, I reflected on how sad that was. He was working towards what he really wanted and now he would never have that chance.

"Could losing the weight have put some strain on his heart?" I wondered aloud.

"From the looks of it he had only just started a day or too earlier. There was no way he had lost enough weight to cause that kind of issue already," Edwin said, and he would know.

Being a personal trainer, Edwin knew about all the latest fad diets. He came up against them all the time. Edwin was always going on about how people wanted a quick fix. Nobody was interested in doing the hard work over a long period of time.

As we were walking away from the fridge, Crystal bent down. Other than the fact Edwin was admiring her butt, I really didn't see anything.

"What did you find?" I asked.

Crystal came up with a flourish, holding a small flash drive.

"It looks like it fell down the side of the refrigerator," she said.

At that moment we heard footsteps in the house and looking over we saw Griffin and Ramos in the doorway, pointing guns at us. Crystal, proving her ability to think quickly no matter what the situation, dropped the flash drive between her breasts and turned around with her hands up and a smile on her face.

Griffin dropped his gun to his side and started to holster it. "What the hell are you doing here?" he snarled.

Assuming that level of rudeness was directed at me, I tried to think of something to say that he wouldn't know was a complete lie.

"I got nothing," I said, looking at Crystal and Edwin.

Crystal looked horrified as if she couldn't believe that she was friends with someone so completely useless when it came to lying. Dropping her head, she took a deep breath.

"Adam Hendricks lent me a key as I left something here the last time I came," she said. "You can call him if you want. You might also want to explain what you are doing here. My understanding was that all police were supposed to have been cleared out of here and I'm guessing you don't have a warrant." She smiled sweetly.

See what I mean, lethal. I am so glad she is on my side. Although from the look I got from her earlier, I knew that I was going to get a very long lecture on the fact that I needed to learn to lie on my feet.

Griffin's jaw tightened.

"Neighbor saw you in here and gave us a call," Ramos said. "There were concerns you were robbing the place."

"So they sent Homicide cops to a suspected break in," Crystal said, sarcasm dripping from every word. "My, if that is all you guys have to do I'm feeling safer in this city already."

I looked at Crystal incredulously. I've seen her in action before but sometimes I think she pushes it a bit too far. Looking at Edwin, I knew I couldn't rely on him to help me with her. When Crystal went into this mood he reacted like Pavlov's dog, drooling and ready to do whatever she wanted him to do. Crystal and Griffin stared at each other, their mutual loathing pretty much evident for all to see.

"I think we've looked everywhere, Crystal," I said in a small voice, stepping in front of her to cut the line of animosity between the two of them. Oh great, now they were both mad at me. "I don't think we're going to find it."

Edwin grabbed Crystal's arm and with me on the other side we led her towards the front entrance with Griffin and Ramos behind us.

Ramos hung up her phone. "Just spoke to Adam Hendricks, they've got permission to be here."

"Well of course I do," said Crystal, with all the confidence of someone who was always in the right. "Now, could you please leave so I can lock up."

The two detectives went through the door with Griffin giving me a hard look. Oh, I could just tell I'd made it back to his people who annoy him list. That was just wonderful.

"I need to go to the bathroom," Crystal said quickly and hurried back into the house.

Edwin followed her with a concerned look on his face. I would have gone too but I was stopped by the hand on my elbow. Looking down at it, I saw Griffin had a tight grip and wasn't likely to let me go. Ramos had headed back to their car and was leaning against it, watching the two of us.

"Care to tell me what's going on?" he asked.

"Not really," I said. "Just spending a day with friends and we ended up here on an errand. Like Ramos said, we had keys and we had permission. The cops had got everything they wanted from this place didn't they?"

"Just finding it interesting that you turned up here on the day you ditch me."

Oh right, I'd forgotten about our little phone call this morning.

"I'm sorry about the way I acted this morning," I said. "I didn't have any right to be so rude to you."

Griffin looked surprised. Maybe he didn't get apologies very often. Considering the abrasive way he seemed to be with people, I was pretty sure that most of the time people didn't feel like he deserved an apology. I did though. I didn't feel good about what I'd said to him on the phone.

"Don't worry about it," he said gruffly. At that moment Crystal and Edwin reappeared and I was close to kissing them.

"Ready to go?" she queried, locking the door.

"Don't get involved in this," Griffin said to me.

"Thanks to you, I'm already involved up to my neck," I said.

"I know," he said awkwardly, "and I'm sorry about that."

I thought about that sentence all the way home. The thing is, he really looked sorry that I was involved. That was strange considering how much of this was his fault.

Chapter Fourteen

"So, what was Detective Hottie talking to you about?" asked Edwin. "He looked kind of intense,"

"Oh, he always looks intense," I said. "I think it's his go to face."

"Nice to look at," mused Crystal. "Wonder what he'd be like in the sack?"

I could feel the blush rising up my face and I prayed neither of them was looking at me.

"Oh my God." Crystal wrenched her head around and almost drove us off the road.

"Will you watch the road, please," I cried out as my hands slammed against the dash.

I'd almost died in a car crash once and I have had a major fear about cars ever since. I follow the speed limit and the road rules like they are the Ten Commandments.

"I'm sorry," Crystal said with chagrin.

She knows what I'm like with driving and the reason why. She pulled into a shop parking area and turned to me as I went through my own version of a panic attack.

Edwin rubbed the back of my shoulders while Crystal kept repeating "I'm sorry, I'm sorry," with a devastated look on her face.

I know the way I feel about cars and driving is not anyone's fault. Except the jerk who decided getting in a car after binge drinking for four straight hours was a great way to end the night. Edwin and Crystal know this and usually when I am in the car they call it their granny mode. Every road rule is meticulously followed because they can see my knuckles whiten if they stray anywhere away from those rules. They are the only ones who know how badly I was affected.

Between the two of them I managed to calm down

enough to gasp out. "I'm sorry, I didn't mean to panic like that."

"No," Crystal said, and I hated that she was so distraught because of my issues. "I should have been paying more attention to what I was doing."

"I'm okay to go on now," I said, breathing in deeply.

"Hell no," said Edwin, still rubbing my shoulders. "You are going to tell us why you went bright red when Crystal was talking about Detective Hottie in bed."

Right, that was why we were here. I'd kind of forgotten that part in the middle of my panic mode. Edwin and Crystal were looking at me expectantly.

"Yesterday he was at the wake and he was trying not to be noticed. He kissed me to hide his face."

"Kissed you to hide his face," Crystal repeated. "He's a cop and that's the best he could come up with."

I blushed again.

"Was he any good at least?" Crystal asked.

At that I dropped my head as I felt my face get even hotter.

"I think we have our answer," said Edwin softly.

Crystal laughed as she started up the car again and we headed home. Once inside my apartment I grabbed my laptop. Crystal went diving down the front of her top looking for the flash drive and Edwin sat back, grabbed a drink and enjoyed the show. Loading up the flash drive, I started clicking open files and found photos of Adam Hendricks and Emily Saunders doing what I caught them doing last night.

"Oh my God. Did you know about this?" Crystal asked, looking at me accusingly.

I grimaced, "I walked in on them during the wake last night."

"Having sex," said Edwin.

"Yes."

"During a wake," said Crystal.

"Yes."

Crystal slapped me on the arm, hard. "And you didn't tell me straight away."

"I didn't get in until after three," I complained, rubbing my arm. "You know for such a tiny person you hit really hard."

She hit me again. "Any time of the day or night, you have permission to call me if you have information like that." I got hit again.

"Stop hitting me," I complained, glaring at her.

Looking to Edwin for support was no good. "I agree with her, that information is too good to keep from everybody else," he said.

Rubbing my sore and I'm sure bruised arm, I kept clicking through the images. They weren't the best quality photos but considering the subject matter I was thinking I should be thankful for small mercies.

"Do we know who sent them to Ryan?" asked Edwin.

"It might have been a private investigator he hired," I guessed.

"No," said Crystal. "A private investigator would have better equipment for getting these images. These look like a camera phone has been used to take the shots."

Flicking through to the last file, I found it was a video and I looked at Edwin and Crystal.

"Do we really want to see this?" I asked.

It was one thing to see photos of the two of them in various states of happiness, but after last night I didn't think I was ready for a moving visual again.

"Of course," chorused Edwin and Crystal, both of them grinning. I opened the file and I've got to say I was surprised. The screen filled with the face of a teenage boy. He looked young and small but he had that cocky arrogance of someone who is not going to let the world get them down.

"Hello Ryan. My name is Roberto. As you can see, I have some pretty interesting photos that I have been taking lately. I could make a lot of money from them. Or you and I can sit down and maybe have a discussion about them. I'll contact you again."

The three of us sat there looking at the screen.

"Ryan Hendricks was being blackmailed," Edwin said.

"It doesn't make sense," I said. "Wouldn't it be better to blackmail Adam or Emily? Adam might not have the money he wants, but Emily is a trust fund baby. She could pay this kid off with what she finds in the bottom of her purse."

"Maybe he wanted something else," ventured Edwin.

"I think I've seen this kid before," I said, desperately searching my memory.

"Really?" asked Crystal. "Where would you have seen him?"

"I don't know." I couldn't work it out, the kid's face was bugging me. I was sure I had seen it somewhere. Long after Crystal and Edwin left, I lay awake in my bed trying to remember.

Chapter Fifteen

For the first time in months there were no demands on my phone from Eleanor the next morning. Once I'd had my coffee and a shower, I sat down at my laptop and had another look at the video, trying desperately to place the kid. I was sure I had seen him before. I started searching. For the next several hours I trawled through all the social media and gossip sites that I knew of. When I finally found him I couldn't help but feel a bit smug. I knew I'd seen him before. He had been hanging around on the outskirts of some of the paparazzi packs which stalked stars like Eleanor Channing. I saw them so much they had become like the scenery in the background. From what I could remember this kid was new. I remember thinking at the time he was out of his league, but there he was.

Once I worked out where I'd seen him, I needed to find out where he was. Looking at the video, the guy obviously thought of himself as a bit of an entrepreneur. He had the whole cocky swagger going. In this day and age every kid was on social media and if he thought he was going to crack it in the paparazzi big leagues, he was going to have to get his name out there. I mean, look at the name he gave. Roberto. The kid was skinny with freckles and red hair. I was pretty sure Roberto wasn't his real name. In that case he'd decided to create a brand.

Hollywood is a town where everything is about your brand. This kid lived here and I would bet money he was absorbing everything that he could learn about this place. Part of that would be his brand, so I went hunting for it. After going through every site I could find, I finally found him. He'd been sending in photos with the GPS coordinates on them this morning. Those photos told me that our mystery photographer was, at this very moment, looking out over Venice Beach. I closed the laptop with a satisfying click and smiled. I needed to have a talk with Roberto and now I knew where to find him.

Venice Beach was a little quieter than usual. When I got the chance I enjoyed coming down here. It didn't take long for me to find the young boy taking random shots with his phone. I sat down on the bench beside him.

"Hello, Roberto," I said. He looked like he was about to run.

"I'm not here to hurt you, I just want to talk," I said.

"What do you want?" the kid asked with the kind of bravado that only a teenager can muster.

"I want to know about how you know Ryan Hendricks and why you were blackmailing him."

"I wasn't blackmailing him," Roberto said defensively. "We were just trying to work out what the situation was and how we could make it work for our mutual benefit. Why lady, are you looking at getting in on the action too?"

I looked at him and all of a sudden I felt old.

"Hey kid, when did you eat last?" I asked.

"I'm fine," he said, but his eyes had lit up.

"Let's get you some food and then maybe we can have a talk," I said.

We found a little diner and the two of us settled into our booth.

"What can I have?" asked Roberto, and I couldn't help but feel bad at the fact that he felt he needed to ask that question.

"Just have what you want from the menu," I said. "I'll cover it."

Roberto put down the menu. "What exactly am I going to be doing to pay for this meal?" he asked, suspicion in his eyes.

Okay, that made me feel lousy. How many times had this kid had to ask that question? I wanted to give him a hug but realized that any physical contact at this stage was not going to be welcome.

"Nothing," I said. "I have some questions about the photos you took that you sent to Ryan Hendricks, but you can choose whether to answer those questions. If you would prefer, you can have your meal and we will talk later. If you don't like the questions I am asking or you just don't want to talk about it, you can walk out of here, no harm, no foul."

"Okay," he said.

He then proceeded to order a massive meal that made me worry that he was going to be really sick by the end of it. Table manners seemed to come in secondary to the need to put as much food into his mouth as necessary. I touched him on the back of his hand softly to get his attention.

"There isn't a time limit," I said. "We can stay here a while if you want to take it slower." He grunted at me but slowed down. I had a brother so I knew how much a teenage boy was capable of eating. After what seemed like forever, Roberto sat back with a satisfied look on his face.

"So," I asked, "are you going to stay and talk?"

He stretched his arms out behind his head.

"Sure, babe," he said.

I cocked my head. "Don't call me babe. I really don't like it."

He grinned at me and in that moment I saw the cheeky spirit that he had.

"What's your real name?" I blurted out.

Not on the list of questions that we had but all of a sudden it seemed to be important to me that I knew who this kid was. Roberto looked disconcerted.

"I'm not going to turn you in to anybody," I said. "I just want to know who I'm talking to."

Roberto looked around and in that moment I could see uncertainty. "My name is Roberto," he maintained stubbornly.

"Any last name, Roberto?" I sighed, willing to accept what he was saying, at least temporarily.

"Not that I'm giving you at the moment," he said.

Okay, boundaries had been set.

"When did you get those photos that you sent to Ryan?" I asked.

"A couple of weeks ago," he said. "I was just hanging and I saw them together. No one else was around and I saw the woman and knew she was Ryan Hendricks's girl. She pretty much had her hand down that guy's pants in the middle of the street so I thought I'd follow them."

"Taking photos of them having sex seemed like a good idea?" I asked.

"Course it did. I bet you would have done the same thing," Roberto said defensively.

"Honestly, I've got to say, I also walked in on them having sex and my first instinct was to get the hell out, not to whip out a camera phone and go all art house porno on them."

"You've got to get in the game," Roberto said.

"No, I really don't," I said. "Why did you go to Ryan with the blackmail instead of Emily? She'd probably have deeper pockets and more reason to pay up."

"I didn't go to him to blackmail him," Roberto said indignantly.

"Then why did you go to him?"

"I thought he should know that his old lady was stepping out on him and what the guy was like. What?"

He'd caught my smile which I was working very hard to quash.

"You were trying to do the right thing," I said.

"I was not." Roberto sounded defensive. "I just thought maybe he could help me with an exclusive one day if I did a solid by him."

"No." I shook my head. "You gave up a guaranteed payday to help someone out. That says something about you."

I grinned broadly at him. He slumped back in the booth, crossed his arms and if he'd been a little bit younger he would probably have poked his tongue out at me.

"I spoke to the dude a couple of times. He didn't seem too broken up about it, so we just kind of left it at that. Heard he died last week so I figured the whole thing was over and done with. Why are you asking questions?"

He stopped and went rigid as if he had a sudden thought.

"Are you a cop?"

"No, why do I act like one?"

"Nah, you're too nice to be a cop. Cops kind of get too focused and go over the top of people to get what they want."

"Don't I know it," I said, thinking of one particular cop. "Well thanks, Roberto," I said as I got up. "You've been a real help."

"Are you sure that's all you need?" he asked, his voice suddenly small. I sat back down.

"Do you want me to take you somewhere?" I asked.

"Nah, I'm good," he said, pulling his bravado around him.

"Do you have a home to go to, Roberto?" I asked gently.

Roberto's head dropped. "No, my mom's new boyfriend kicked me out last week. Said I was useless and he didn't want me sponging off him anymore. Mom let him do it."

In that moment my heart broke a bit.

"Where have you been staying?" I asked.

"Here and there." He avoided my eyes.

"How old are you, Roberto?" I asked.

"I'm sixteen," he said. "Plenty old enough to be on my own."

There it was again. He tried to act and look tough but all I could see was a teenage kid who looked younger than he was. The thought of what could happen to him on the streets, what may have already happened to him, broke my heart. In that moment I decided on a course of action that

Griffin would have called boneheaded.

"Come home with me. It isn't much but I can offer you a warm place to sleep on my couch and food, just for tonight. We'll try to work out someplace for you to go which is safe after that."

"Why would you do that?" he said, his eyes wary.

"Because if you were a puppy I'd have loaded you in the car by now and taken you home. You think I'm going to do less for you than if you were a puppy."

He cocked his head, very puppy like behavior I thought, as he considered what I was offering. He may also have been trying to work out the safest way to get away from the crazy woman who invited street kids into her home.

"What do you want in return?" he asked, his eyes narrowed.

"I don't want anything from you," I said. "Just get a good night's sleep where you can feel safe and then tomorrow you can go where you like."

"You know lady, you are nuts," he said. "Do you know how dangerous it is to open your home to some strange homeless kid?"

"Actually I do," I said. Pretty much everybody, including my cop fake boyfriend, would be appalled. Sometimes the right thing is taking a chance based on instincts, and my instincts were telling me that Roberto was a good kid who was having a rough time.

"Look, it's your choice. I'm just offering a place to stay for the night. If you're looking to steal something I'm the wrong person. I've only been in America for a few months. I travel light so unless you think you can get a good price for cheap sensible shoes on the black market, I'm not a good mark. I'm not going to try to sell this to you. I'm giving you a choice, just like I gave you the choice to walk out before. I'm leaving now. You can come with me if you want."

As I left the booth, I could see that he was hesitating.

After getting abandoned by his own mother, I didn't hold out much hope for him believing a stranger was willing to help. I wasn't going to beg him to take my help. By the time I got to the door he was behind me.

"Good choice," I murmured.

"I certainly hope so," he said.

Chapter Sixteen

As we got in the car I turned to him.

"Before we start this," I said, "we need names, real names."

Roberto looked at me silently. "Sean Boylan," he mumbled.

I stuck out my hand and gripped his for a handshake. "Pleased to meet you, Sean Boylan. I'm Trudie Eyre and for the next twenty-four hours you abide by my rules."

"Like what?" he complained as he put on his seat belt.

I started up the car. "In my house there are no drugs, no alcohol and no cigarettes."

"You don't get laid very often do you?" Sean said.

"You will remember you are staying with a lady and your language and conversation will reflect that," I said primly with a small smile on my face. Out of the corner of my eye I could see Sean smiling as well. "Thanks for reminding me though, there will be no young ladies invited into my house, in fact no friends at all. Music volume is down unless you're wearing headphones in which case I really don't care as you are ruining your own hearing not mine."

"You've got kids don't you?" said Sean.

"No," I said, "but I used to work as a nanny."

"That explains it," he said. "You've got that whole uptight thing going on. I'm guessing you don't date much at all. That makes it easier, I think a boyfriend would have lost it if you turned up at home with me."

"Yeah, probably would." Lucky for me, fake boyfriends didn't get any say in who I invited back to my home.

Turning up to my apartment, I noticed Crystal knocking on my front door. When I got close, Crystal turned around.

"Where have you been?" she asked, exasperation clear in her voice.

"I worked out how to find the person who took the photos and went to meet him," I said.

"That's great," she exclaimed. "Did you get any information?"

"Some, it seems Ryan Hendricks wasn't really all that fussed about the fact that his brother was sharing time with his fiancée."

"Why were any of these people involved with each other?" Crystal asked. "Why don't they just get laid and move on? Clean and simple. Some people are just not meant for monogamy and the sooner they realize that the happier everyone would be."

Noticing Sean's inordinate interest in the conversation I moved to quieten Crystal.

"What did you want me for?" I asked.

"I need to return the key to Ryan's house to Adam. He just called and sounded kind of panicked. Said he needed the keys now. Just wanted to know if you want to come with me."

"That would be great," I said, then remembered that I had Sean and I wasn't going to take him anywhere near Adam. At this stage I did not know if Adam knew about Sean, but if he did I wanted to keep them apart.

"I can't right now," I said, looking at Sean.

Crystal pulled me aside, out of earshot. "Who's he?"

"It's the kid who took the photos of Adam and Emily. He got tossed out of home and has nowhere to stay. I'm letting him sleep at my place tonight and tomorrow I'll find someplace else for him."

I looked down at her, expecting a lecture on what a stupid idea that was, and was surprised to see the shimmer of tears in her eyes. She threw her arms around me and muttered into my shoulder. "That's the reason I love you."

"Are you gay?" asked Sean, "Because it's okay if you are, I'm just asking because I gotta say, this is looking a little hot."

I rolled my eyes thinking I would never understand men. Crystal pulled away, surreptitiously wiping her eyes.

"No we're not gay but I need Trudie for a little bit."

"Oh, that's fine. I can find someplace else to go."

"No you're not," I said as I grabbed his arm when he turned around and started to walk off.

"Miss Betsy," I yelled across the complex, getting her attention.

The elderly lady looked tired as she was weeding a part of the garden which had been neglected a bit lately.

"Sorry dear," she said. "I haven't had much of a chance to tidy this area. We've had quite a few maintenance issues lately so the garden has gone to the bottom of my to do list."

"So you're going to be gardening all day today?" I asked.

"Pretty much all day," she said.

I pulled Sean forward. "I've got a friend staying with me today but I need someone to keep an eye on him while I go out. I am sure he would be thrilled to help you for the day."

I could see the mutinous look in Sean's eyes and dropped my voice. "Please give her a hand. The work is hard on her."

His expression softened as he looked over the elderly lady with dirt encrusted on her hands. "Sure I'll help."

"That would be lovely," said Miss Betsy.

"Wait here," I said to Crystal.

Racing into my apartment I grabbed a cap and some sunscreen. Coming out I passed them to Sean. He looked at me strangely.

"Look, I come from Australia, the skin cancer capital of the world, and that red hair and pale skin scream disaster to me. Put on the hat and the sunscreen and don't question it."

"You are one weird chick," mumbled Sean as he

jammed the cap on.

I smiled at him proudly. "I know," I said as I followed Crystal to the car.

"You know he's right," she said as we were driving. "You are kind of strange."

"Why?" I asked.

"You've got this whole maternal, take care of everyone vibe and yet you don't have any of your own children or anything close to a relationship."

"You're forgetting my fake boyfriend."

"Ah yes, Detective Hottie. Have you heard from him lately?"

"Not since yesterday at Ryan's house. I don't think he was too happy with me. Because he's only my fake boyfriend, I'm not even sure if he's giving me his version of the silent treatment."

Crystal giggled. "You get yourself into the strangest situations," she said as we pulled into the driveway at Adam's house.

As we got out of the car, we heard a crash coming from inside the house. The front door of the house smashed open. Crystal and I dove back in the car as two men came out, dragging a struggling Adam Hendricks between them. Seeing us, one of the men raised a gun and started shooting at the car. Crystal threw the car in reverse and started driving away from the scene. Both of us ducked below the dashboard as shots were fired in our direction. I grabbed my cell and called 911. When someone answered I started yelling into the phone.

"Some guy is shooting at us."

"Ma'am where are you?"

I looked at Crystal. I didn't know where we were. I'd just been the passenger, I hadn't actually been paying attention to the address or anything. Crystal yelled out an address as I held the phone to her.

"Did you get that?" I asked.

The gunshots stopped and Crystal and I looked over

the dashboard. Adam was being pushed into the car. As he struggled, he was hit by a meaty fist to the jaw and he slumped.

"Ma'am are you still there?" the calm voice from the 911 operator came through and I realized that in the midst of all this drama, Crystal and I had gone silent.

"I'm here," I said.

The other car drove past us, wheels squealing and shots again rang out. Crystal pushed her foot hard on the accelerator and sent the car forward out of the range of the gunfire. She wrenched the car around and started chasing after them.

"What the hell?" I yelled out.

"They've taken Adam. Tell the cops, maybe they can intercept them."

I took a deep breath. "My name is Trudie Eyre. I've been working with Detective Jake Griffin. Adam Hendricks was just kidnapped from his house at the address we gave you. The men who took him were the ones shooting at us. We are chasing the kidnapper's car, going south now."

"Ma'am, I don't think that is a good idea. If they have already been shooting at you they are dangerous. You should stop now and find somewhere safe."

I was inclined to agree with the nice man on the phone. Unfortunately, I was not the one in charge of the wheel. Crystal was getting us close to the kidnapper's vehicle. I felt a huge crunch as the kidnapper's car swerved into us and we were pushed into a car parked on the side of the road. Airbags went off and I've got to tell you, they aren't gentle. They may look like pillows but those things hurt. My chest felt like it had taken a hit from a baseball bat. We weren't going anywhere. In the distance I heard police sirens coming close and the kidnapper's car reversed away from us. In a cloud of smoke and squealing wheels, it took off in the opposite direction. Looking over at Crystal, I saw blood dripping down her forehead.

"Oh no, Crystal," I said as I put my hand to her cheek. "Are you okay?"

"Yeah," she said, although she sounded a little groggy. "Not sure what I hit my head on though." She winced as she raised her hand to her hairline.

A police officer came up to the window on my side. "Are you okay?"

"I think so," I said, "but my friend's hurt. Did you get the guys that hit us?"

"No, we have another car that has gone after them. Can you hold on there for a few minutes? Paramedics should be here soon."

Before too long we were out of the car and heading to hospital. I was sitting on the bed in a hospital room after having my statement taken by the nice young policeman when Crystal came in.

"I'm sorry," she said as she sat on the edge of my bed. "I should never have done that."

"You're more hurt than me." I pointedly looked at the bandage on her forehead.

"Yes, but I know how you feel about cars. I probably made things worse."

"On the plus side," I said, trying very hard to put an end to the guilt she was obviously feeling, "my constant nagging about wearing seat belts was totally worth it."

Crystal giggled and winced as it pulled on the edges of the bandage. "I guess it was."

We looked up at a knock on the door. Standing there with a concerned look on his face was Griffin.

"Finally," I said. "It's about time my fake boyfriend turned up."

"Yeah," said Griffin. "I figured I'd better put in an appearance. Could we have a moment please, Crystal? Ramos is out there. She wants to have a chat with you."

"No problem," said Crystal and left the room. Griffin was looking at me strangely.

"I'm fine," I said.

"No, you're not," he said. "You could have been killed today. What the hell were you thinking?"

"We were returning the key to Ryan's house. Trust me, there was no way I could have known we were walking into that," I said indignantly. "Did you have some information that indicated he was going to get kidnapped?"

"No," he said. "I had no idea."

"See," I said triumphantly. "Neither of us are fortune tellers. I could have just as easily walked into an armed holdup or a drive by shooting."

"Are you trying to make me feel better or worse?" he said. Leaning over he tucked my hair behind my ear. "Do you have any idea how hard it was to get that message from dispatch and know there was nothing I could do to help? Knowing the danger you were in."

I knew he was saying something important but at that moment I was losing myself in those beautiful green eyes.

"I feel like this is somehow my fault," he murmured.

"That's because it is your fault," came an officious voice from behind.

Griffin straightened to face the wrath of Monique.

"She shouldn't be anywhere near this situation but you forced her into it."

Oh boy, was Monique mad. In heels she stood eye to eye with Griffin and she was letting him have it. Strangely enough, Griffin was just taking it. Unlike when he was talking to me his face had tightened up and that cold mask of his had come over it.

"Monique," I said, trying to break into the tirade, because once Monique got started she could go for days.

Monique looked over at me.

"Let it go," I said. "Please." I may have also put a hand to my head, intimating that I had a headache to elicit a bit of sympathy. Sometimes you had to use everything you had.

"For you, ma petite, I will do that," she said as she

moved towards me on the bed, gripping hold of my hand.

"I'll see you later, Trudie," Griffin said as he made his exit.

"You had to scare him off didn't you?" I said to Monique, shaking my head.

"He is no good for you," announced Monique imperiously.

Reggie, who had followed her in, sat on the other side of the bed. "How are you feeling, sweetheart?" he asked solicitously.

"I'm fine," I said. "The only reason I'm here is we're waiting for the x-rays on my ribs. I felt a little bit of pain earlier and they're just being careful about it."

"Crystal's pretty upset that she put you through that," Monique said quietly.

"Please tell me you didn't have a go at her as well," I implored Monique.

"Of course not," she said, as if offended I would say such a thing. "I like Crystal."

Chapter Seventeen

Pulling up to the apartment complex, I noted that Sean was still in the garden working with Miss Betsy. I groaned. The poor kid. I had not meant for him to be working all day. After saying goodbye to Monique and Reggie, and making sure Crystal got dropped off with Edwin, I went back to the garden.

"Hey, Miss Betsy," I said as I came to her side. "Is it time to let him go for the day?"

"He's a good boy, worked hard," she said. "You did the right thing bringing him here. We'll take care of him."

Obviously Miss Betsy had managed to get Sean's story out of him. I wondered if he realized that he may never be able to leave now.

"Want something to eat, Sean?" I asked.

He looked at me gratefully. "I'll just finish this and be right in," he said.

"See," Miss Betsy said quietly, "a good boy."

Back in my apartment, I started getting things ready for my house guest. Despite the number of times I seemed to eat takeaway, I can cook and I decided that tonight Sean needed something homemade. I had the sauce for a pasta dish bubbling away on the stove when he walked in. I caught a whiff of pungent, sweaty teenage boy and wrinkled my nose.

"Do you have any clean clothes?" I asked.

"Not really," he said, lifting up his arm to sniff.

I went into my room and grabbed some sweats and a t-shirt of mine that looked like it would kind of fit.

"Take a shower and throw your clothes out. Give me everything you have and I'll get them washed."

While Sean was in the shower I ran downstairs into the laundry room and threw his clothes in the machine. Back upstairs I had to laugh at how discomfited Sean looked in my clothes. They didn't look obviously feminine but you could tell that they offended his sense of masculinity.

"Don't be such a guy," I said as I dished up some dinner for him.

After settling Sean on the couch, I went to bed. Despite the dramas of the day I was grateful when I fell into a deep, dreamless sleep.

I woke up in the morning a bit disoriented. Noises coming from outside my bedroom filled me with alarm until I remembered my house guest. Stumbling out of my bedroom I was a bit concerned when I found Sean at the kitchen bench on my laptop.

"I hope you don't mind me using your computer," he said.

Crossing my arms, I fixed him with a cold stare.

"Actually I do," I said. "I've got a bit of a thing for privacy."

"Probably shouldn't tell you about going through your medicine cabinet should I?" he said with a cheeky grin on his face.

"You've got the self-preservation instincts of a lemming," I said sarcastically, as I went to grab my laptop.

"Yeah, I know," he said. "Where are the rest of the photos?"

"What do you mean the rest of the photos?"

"After I met with Ryan he paid me a few bucks to keep an eye on his brother. I got a few other photos but they weren't with the chick. They were with some guy. I gave those to Ryan as well."

"We only found one flash drive with the photos of Adam and Emily. Do you still have copies of the other images?" I asked.

"Sure," said Sean. "I already downloaded them to your laptop."

I opened up the laptop and started to go through the photos. My heart sank. There, in irrefutable color, was

Adam Hendricks buying drugs, doing drugs and partying with guys that scared me just looking at their photos. This was not good and all of a sudden I started to see that this situation had got worse, and this sixteen year old kid was now in the middle of it.

"Sean, does anyone else know you took these photos?" I asked, as the ramifications of this situation swirled through my head.

"I didn't tell anyone, but Ryan might have said something to someone," Sean said, seemingly oblivious to the sudden tension emanating from me.

"Sean, I need you to listen to me. This is a bad situation." I pointed to Adam. "Yesterday I saw this guy being kidnapped by this guy here." I pointed to one of the men in the photo. "He and another guy shot at Crystal and me. They then ran us off the road."

Sean looked horrified.

"We need to take this to the police," I said.

Sean started to argue.

"No, Sean," I said in as firm a voice as I could. "These are bad people and if they find out that you took these photos it is going to put you in a lot of danger."

"I could just leave," Sean said, grabbing his backpack. "You'll be safe then."

I grabbed one of the straps on his backpack.

"This isn't about me, you idiot," I said. "I don't want you hurt. We need to come up with a way to keep you safe."

Sean looked stunned. "You're trying to take care of me," he said softly.

"Somebody has to," I said, pointing a finger at his chest. "Self-preservation instincts of a lemming remember. I have a friend, kind of, who's a cop. He'll be able to help us. I can call him now and we can get him to have a look at these. He'll know the next step to take."

Sean nodded and sat down heavily. Dialing Griffin's number, I hoped I had made the right decision.

"Griffin," he answered, and I had to admit that just hearing his voice was enough to make me feel better.

"Griffin, it's Trudie."

"Hey, Trudie." His voice softened and I tried really hard not to read anything into that.

"I have a problem," I said hurriedly. "I want to tell you about this problem but I need to know that you are going to think carefully before bulldozing forward with the whole cop thing."

"What's going on, Trudie?" Griffin growled.

"Some information has fallen into my lap which may, and I do stress only may, be pertinent to the Ryan Hendricks situation. I think it's the reason Adam got kidnapped yesterday."

"Where are you?" growled Griffin.

"I'm at home."

"I'm coming over now." Griffin hung up on me.

Turning around I turned off my phone. "He'll be here soon." Looking down at myself in my old worn pajamas I said ruefully, "I probably should shower and get dressed shouldn't I?"

Sean nodded a little too enthusiastically. I didn't think I looked that bad.

Chapter Eighteen

I only had time to have a quick shower and get dressed before there was a pounding at the door. I wondered if they taught that heavy handed knock at the police academy. As I walked to the door, I threw a reassuring glance at Sean.

"Don't worry, it will be okay. I've got your back remember."

Sean smiled gratefully. Admittedly, it was a really tense kind of smile but I was going to put it into the win column.

"You really need to lighten up on the knocking," I said as I opened the door.

Griffin walked in, slowing down as he spotted Sean.

"Where's Ramos?" I asked, looking behind him.

"Considering what you said on the phone I thought it was a good idea to keep her out of it until I see what we are dealing with."

He was talking to me but his eyes were completely fastened on Sean. Sean for his part looked ready to bolt, and personally I didn't blame him. I'd been on the receiving end of Griffin's glares. I could appreciate Sean's need to be anywhere else. I walked over to Sean and put an arm around his shoulder, partly in support and partly to make sure he didn't run.

"This is Sean, I met him yesterday."

"And you let him stay here last night," Griffin said incredulously.

I stopped. "How did you know that?"

"Detective, remember."

I looked around. I had to admit, the made up couch was kind of a giveaway.

"Sean is the one who has something to say."

The three of us sat down and Sean told Griffin everything about taking the photos, going to Ryan Hendricks and about how we ended up in the place where we were right now. I kept my eyes on Griffin and could see his jaw get tighter and tighter. When he saw the last of the photos and I pointed out the man I'd seen at Adam's kidnapping yesterday, he ran his hand over his face.

"You've both well and truly stepped in it haven't you?" he asked, with what I'm assuming was a rhetorical question. I'm not a cop and even I could see we were in trouble.

He pointed to the photo of the guy who was handing Adam what looked like some pills.

"This here is Vincent Mendoza. He is the nephew of Johnny Rollins, one of the big guys in the illegal drug trade in LA. Vincent is a bit of an idiot but he is the only child of Johnny's much loved older sister. Johnny has had to pull this moron out of the fire more than once and people have a tendency to get very hurt when Johnny is protecting family. The guy you identified as one of the kidnappers yesterday is part of Johnny's crew." Looking at me he said regretfully, "I'm sorry, Trudie. I can't deal with this alone. It is way too big. If Ryan Hendricks confronted Adam about these photos and Adam told Mendoza, he could have been killed in any number of ways. The tox screen was clear for drugs but there could be something there that is new that we don't have a test for."

I nodded. "Sean, this is your life we're talking about. You get a say in this as well."

Sean looked surprised but there was no way I was going to let Griffin take this choice away from him. I was surprised to realize that it looked like I still had some residual anger in me regarding the way Griffin had treated me. Looking at Griffin, I could see that he saw that as well.

"Ryan Hendricks is dead because of the photos I took," Sean said quietly.

"No," I said vehemently, putting my arms around him

and pulling him into a hug that I probably needed just as much as he did. "Ryan Hendricks may still have died from natural causes. Even if he didn't and these guys killed him, you are not responsible, they are." I said it fiercely, not wanting him to hold onto that guilt.

"The right thing would be to help the cops wouldn't it?" he said quietly.

"Probably," I said reluctantly.

"Do you think they'll keep me safe?" he asked.

"I think," I said, choosing my words carefully, "that Detective Griffin is a good cop. I think that he will do everything that he can to protect you."

The last was said looking over Sean's head at Griffin, pleading with him not to make a liar of me.

Griffin nodded and that seemed to be enough for Sean.

Griffin got on the phone to Ramos. Once he'd finished the conversation he turned to Sean and me.

"Alright, the way we're going to play this is that you are going to give me those photos. As of this moment you are an anonymous source. I am going to try to keep your name out of this."

"Thanks, Griffin," I said quietly.

"Don't thank me yet. At this stage we don't know how much information the bad guys have on you. Adam's kidnapping is not my case. I'm supposed to have nothing to do with it. Ramos is going to swing by for the photos and then she and I are going to do some hunting and we'll see if we can get a better handle on what's going on."

While waiting for Ramos, Sean decided he wanted to do some more work in the garden with Miss Betsy. As he was leaving I pulled him aside and indicated to Griffin that I needed some privacy.

"How are you going with all this?" I asked.

"Not a problem," he said, with what I was thinking was more of his teenage hyped bravado.

"Really?" I asked with a skeptical look on my face.

"Yeah, maybe not so much," he conceded, once again

looking like a scared boy.

"Griffin will help you." I tried to sound reassuring. "He's a good guy."

I looked over at Griffin as he picked up the photo I had of my brother and sister.

"So if you're Gertrude, are these Norman and Hildegarde?"

"Your name is Gertrude," snorted Sean as he tried to contain his laughter.

Walking over to Griffin I wrenched the photo out of his hand.

Looking at his smirking face I called out to Sean as he was walking out the door, "I've changed my mind, he isn't a good guy."

Griffin laughed and lowered his voice. "Oh, honey, I'm very good."

Flustered, I put the photo back down.

"Their names are Jamie and Katie. Mom learned her lesson after me and refused to name them until after she was out of hospital and had forgotten the pain and the drugs."

Griffin picked up another photo of my whole family which had been taken when on holiday.

"You look like you have a happy family."

I smiled as I looked at the photo.

"I do. None of us is perfect but we fit well together. My parents adore each other and they love us. My sister Katie wants to be an actress so she thinks I have the coolest job in the world. She always wants to hear about everything that happens to me. Jamie is still in school but he'll be finishing up soon. Sean reminds me of him a bit."

"Is that why you took in a street kid and let him sleep on your couch. Something I might add, which was really stupid."

"Look," I said defensively. "I know it wasn't the smartest idea, but he was alone. I couldn't handle the thought of what could possibly happen to him. Maybe it was about time somebody started caring about him.

Griffin's expression softened. "I just worry about you."

"You're worried about me," I snorted. "You're the guy who was going to get me deported."

"I'm sorry for what I did," Griffin said regretfully. "Forcing you like that was pretty low, I get that now. I didn't mean to hurt you but where I come from, you do what needs to be done. My job is to find the worst people out there. Sometimes I need a reminder that trampling over the innocent to do that isn't the best way. If it makes any difference, if you want to walk away now and have nothing else to do with this, you can. I won't hold the assault charges over you anymore."

"So I could just get you to leave and I would never have to see you again."

"Sure, if that's what you want."

I looked at him, wondering how serious he was. "I'm not walking away," I said softly.

"Good to know," Griffin said.

"So," I asked, "what about your family?"

"Just have my Dad. Mom bailed on us when I was a baby and we haven't seen her since." He shrugged.

"Sorry, I didn't mean to be nosy," I said.

"No more nosy than I was asking about your family."

Ramos came through the open door and stopped suddenly, staring pointedly at Griffin. "Ready to go?" she said.

"Yeah I am." He put his hand gently on my arm. "Remember to stay safe. If Sean comes up with anything else, I want you to call me straight away."

"Sure, of course," I said.

He stopped at the door as if to say something else but then abruptly turned and left.

Chapter Nineteen

A few minutes later Sean came back into the apartment. "Was that Griffin's partner?" he asked.

"Detective Ramos," I said distractedly.

"Man, is she hot," Sean said. "Griffin has got to be nuts if he's not nailing her."

I looked at him carefully.

"Not that you aren't pretty," he said, suddenly remembering who he was talking to. "I mean, not hot like Detective Ramos is, but pretty."

I cocked my head to one side figuring if my looks were going to be savagely critiqued by a teenage boy, I might as well make him feel uncomfortable too.

"I mean you're nice too, really nice and that means more than pretty. I'm sure Detective Griffin is way more interested in nice than…" he trailed off.

"Hot," I supplied.

"Yeah," Sean swallowed, his face downcast.

Feeling sorry for him I laughed. "And what did we just learn?"

"That sometimes I need to keep my big mouth shut," Sean mumbled.

"A very valuable lesson," I nodded wisely.

Sean looked up as his cell indicated he had received a text. He scooped it up, looking pathetically grateful for the distraction.

"What is it?" I asked as his expression changed.

He handed the phone to me and I winced as I looked at a photo of a beaten up Adam Hendricks. The phone vibrated in my hand as it rang.

"What do I do?" Sean asked.

"Answer it on speaker," I said.

"Hello," Sean said tremulously.

The voice coming over the phone sounded harsh and threatening. "Hello, Sean, I want you to listen very carefully. Thanks to Adam here, I know you took some photos of me that I didn't want taken. Now I want you to meet me at the place you took the photos. If you don't, Adam is not going to have a very good time. I know what you're thinking. Why the hell should you care about whether he lives or dies? The thing is, if I don't have those photos by the time he dies, then I have your mother and her boyfriend here as well to fill in the time. Believe me when I say that they will feel a lot of pain before they die. You have half an hour to get here and no telling the cops or you know what will happen."

The phone disconnected suddenly. Another text message came through of a couple who looked as if they had been badly beaten as well.

"My mom," Sean moaned. "What am I going to do?"

"First things first, we're calling Griffin and getting him back here. He'll have a plan for fixing this," I said as I reached for his phone.

Sean put his hand out to stop me. "You heard him, I can't tell the cops or they'll kill my mom."

"The cops can help us," I said urgently. "If you go into this on your own they will kill you. You've seen their faces, you know what they've done. Sean, there is absolutely no reason for you to be kept alive once they've got the photos."

"I can't risk anyone else getting hurt. My little sister is only six years old. She still needs mom, even if I don't."

I could understand perfectly why he wanted to protect his family, but I was going to have to be the grown up here.

"Look, Sean, I need to call Griffin. He's the only one who can help us now."

"Okay," said Sean, resigned to the decision that had been made. "You're right, I can't do this on my own."

"Good," I said. "This is the right decision."

Walking into my bedroom to get my phone, I couldn't believe how much the situation had spiraled out of control. Dialing Griffin's number, I growled in frustration when I could only get his voicemail.

"You need to call me right now. Sean just got a message from Mendoza. He's got Adam, Sean's mom and her boyfriend. They are demanding a swap to get hold of the photos. Call me back now."

"He's not answering," I said as I walked back into the living room to find Sean was no longer there.

"Dammit, Sean," I growled as I raced out of the apartment.

I found Miss Betsy working in the garden again.

"Did Sean come through here?" I asked.

"Why yes, dear," she said as she stood up and wiped the sweat from her forehead. "He took off in your car. I think I'd be careful about lending that car to him. He doesn't seem to be a very good driver."

"Can I borrow your car? I have to stop him. He's about to put himself into a lot of danger. Please," I pleaded.

"Of course, dear," she said. "Do you know where he has gone?"

"No, but my boss has got GPS tracking on the vehicle." I really hoped it was working. As far as I knew Monique had never used it.

"Alright, dear, I'll drive and you direct me and tell me what is going on."

Getting into a car with Miss Betsy has never been one of the things I wanted to do with my life. Miss Betsy's former career as a stuntwoman during a period of history when workplace safety wasn't a priority, leads her to be a little blasé when it comes to the road rules, and some of the laws of the physical universe. I strapped myself in and logged onto the tracking software on my tablet. Following the GPS, Miss Betsy and I found ourselves parked outside an old nightclub. I tried to call Griffin again and this time he answered.

"Where the hell are you?" he growled. "I got your message, I'm back at your place and no one's here."

"Sean took off. He's determined to save his mom." I gave him the address of the nightclub.

"I'm coming right now," Griffin said. "Whatever you are thinking, do not go in there."

I hung up and Miss Betsy looked at me. "We're going in there aren't we?"

"I am going in there," I said. "You stay out here and wait for the cops."

"Oh, sweetie," she said as she patted my cheek. "That is so not going to happen. For one thing, I'm the one with the permit for this."

With that she leaned over and flipped open the glove box. Inside it was the last thing I expected. Miss Betsy pulled out a large black gun.

"What is that?" I squeaked.

She stroked it gently, which I found a whole new level of disturbing.

"It's my baby," she said, "and more importantly it can put a hole through anyone who is trying to hurt that sweet boy."

I contemplated that for a second and you know what, in that moment, I was perfectly okay with that. I would be thinking about that reaction very deeply when I had some time to myself, but that wouldn't be right now.

"How did you want to deal with this?" Miss Betsy asked after tucking the gun into the back of her pants.

"Since you have the weapon I think you should stay behind me and keep a watch until I can have a look around and see what's going on."

As I walked towards the club she grabbed my arm. "It might be smarter to go around the back."

"Why?" I asked.

"Always works out better in the movies."

Great, I was taking my breaking and entering advice from a former stuntwoman carrying a loaded monster of a gun, who was basing her recommendations on movies she had been in. There was no way this was going to end well.

Getting to the back door of the nightclub, I wasn't surprised to find it locked.

"I've got this," Miss Betsy said and pulled a pin from her hair. She proceeded to pick the lock. She turned the doorknob and shrugged as I looked at her in amazement. "You'd be surprised at what you can learn on a movie set."

"When we get out of this," I said, in a rare burst of optimism, "I want you to teach me how to do that."

"If we get out of this," she said, "I'll teach you to shoot as well."

Now I had something to look forward to. We crept along through the kitchen area. Coming to the main area of the nightclub I heard loud voices. Peeking out through a swinging door I saw Sean on the floor, a red mark on his face. Vincent Mendoza was holding his phone. Adam Hendricks was tied to a chair and what looked like Sean's mom and her boyfriend were slumped on the ground next to Sean.

"Tell me the truth or I kill your mother. Has anyone else seen these photos?"

"No," said Sean, obviously terrified. "I promise, I haven't shown them to anyone."

Good, I silently cheered Sean. No need to be honest with the sociopath holding you prisoner. I willed him to say anything that Mendoza wanted to hear. Mendoza was looking through the photos.

"Looks like they're all here," he said. "I don't really need you anymore do I?" he sneered, bringing his gun down and pointing it at Sean.

I dialed Griffin, motioned to Miss Betsy to stay back, sent up a small prayer to St Jude, the patron saint of desperate situations and lost causes, and pushed through the kitchen door. All of a sudden I had two guns pointing in my direction. Mendoza kept his gun aimed at Sean. I put my hands up, holding my phone above my head.

Voice shaking, I said, "I'm here to take Sean home. Let us leave and we can forget about this."

The three thugs looked at me and burst out laughing. Frankly, if I wasn't so terrified, I would have joined them.

"What the hell?" Mendoza said as he moved the gun to point in my direction.

"I am currently on the phone to the LAPD," I said, my voice wavering. "Everything you are doing at the moment is being recorded live. If you kill us you cannot get away with it. They already know that I am standing here with Vincent Mendoza who has a gun aimed at me. If I am killed you will be charged and you will go to jail."

"But you will be dead," Mendoza pointed out.

Yeah, like I hadn't worked out that part of my stupid plan.

"Maybe," I said. "But at that point I won't care. What happens next will cease to matter to me, but what happens next will matter to you very much."

Despite my words, I was terrified. I refused to look at Sean because I didn't know if I could keep this up. My only hope was to delay until Griffin turned up.

"You've put me in a little bit of a situation haven't you," Mendoza said, frowning.

I really hoped so. I needed him to think about his next step very carefully. The longer he took to think it through, the more time that I could give Griffin. I was winging this and I am not a person who works well without a plan. The moment Mendoza had turned the gun on Sean, I hadn't thought of anything but stopping what was coming next. Mendoza came up to me and wrenched the phone out of my hand, cutting the connection to Griffin.

"That takes care of it doesn't it?" he whispered in my ear, the smell of his breath turning my stomach.

"They still know that I'm here with you," I whispered back. "They know that you had a gun on me and they know why I'm here. That is means, motive and opportunity right there, and the recording gives supporting evidence. A prosecuting attorney would love this case."

"You think you're smart don't you?" he sneered, digging that gun into my side.

Actually no. Right at that moment I was thinking that I was a bit of an idiot. I could see my death in Vincent Mendoza's eyes. He badly wanted to hurt me. I really hoped I wasn't shaking as much on the outside as I was on the inside.

All of a sudden I heard voices yelling out. "Police. Freeze. On the floor."

I wrenched myself away from Mendoza and threw myself down, all the time waiting for him to shoot me. My heart beat once, then twice and no shot. Looking up, I saw Mendoza had been thrown to the ground and Griffin had a knee in his back while he was putting handcuffs on him. Other police had taken out the two goons who had kidnapped Adam Hendricks. Still more were attending to Adam and Sean's mom and boyfriend. In a rather undignified way I crawled towards Sean who was watching in shock.

"Are you okay?" I said urgently.

Sean looked at me, his eyes slightly unfocused.

"You stopped him."

"Not really," I said. "That was more of a delaying tactic."

"I can't believe you did that."

"Neither can I," Griffin growled as he grabbed me around my shoulders and hauled me to my feet. "Of all the things you could have done, that was the world's dumbest move."

"I know," I said, leaning into him trying to soak up some warmth.

"You're shaking," he muttered as he put his arms around me.

"I'm really cold," I said.

"Probably shock, and coming down from an adrenalin high."

"Never did understand adrenalin junkies," I said. "This is not pleasant."

"No," he said, his mouth against my hair. "I'm sure you're not finding it particularly pleasant at all."

Sean was behind me and I grabbed hold of his hand.

"I need you to check Sean," I said to Griffin urgently. "I'm too shaky to do it."

"You're amazing," I think I heard him whisper before he let go of me and started making sure Sean was okay.

I wouldn't let go of Sean's hand until the paramedics came and checked us both out. At that point Griffin let Miss Betsy come in to make sure we were okay, before one of the officers arrested her for annoying them. She gave Sean a hug and had him ducking his head in embarrassment.

Moving over to me she looked me in the eyes. "That was the bravest thing I have ever seen.

I lowered my eyes. "I don't feel brave," I said. "I was so scared I thought I was going to throw up."

"Sweetie," she said. "You looked a killer in the face and dared him to kill you to protect that boy. They don't come much braver."

"He's a good kid," I said.

"That he is," she agreed.

"He came here to sacrifice himself for a mother that tossed him out."

"That he did."

"I hope she appreciates it," I said fiercely.

"Oh, Trudie," Miss Betsy said regretfully. "You're looking for a fairy tale ending. From the looks of it, I don't think that is what Sean is going to get."

I looked over at where Sean was talking to his mother and her boyfriend and I had to agree it didn't look good. Sean seemed to be hunching in on himself as his mother was berating him. Dropping the blanket I had wrapped around me, I went over to stand next to him.

"This is all your fault," his mother hissed.

"Hey, wait a minute," I said. "You can't blame him."

"He's my kid you stupid bitch, I can say what I want."

"Don't you call her a bitch," Sean said indignantly.

At that moment I saw out of the corner of my eye the boyfriend raising his hand. I pushed Sean out the way as I realized the punch was heading toward him. Unfortunately, my face ended up where Sean's had been and I caught the punch in the side of my cheek. I heard a blood curdling yell and Miss Betsy jumped on the back of the boyfriend. He swung around trying to dislodge the little old lady who was holding on as if she was at a rodeo. The cops ran over and tried to tackle the man to the ground without hurting the woman on top of him. Sean's mom then decided to tackle the police who were handcuffing her boyfriend. Before we knew it, we were all down at the police station filling in statements.

Chapter Twenty

Once again I was in the interrogation room with Griffin, only this time I was the one with an icepack on my face.

"Do you actually think before you do things?" asked Griffin.

"Usually yes," I said, touching the icepack against my bruised cheek gingerly. "But lately things seem to be getting away from my control. Is Sean okay?"

"He's in the other room talking to Ramos."

Despite the pain I smiled. "That'll make him happy."

"Why is that?" Griffin asked.

"He's a teenage boy and she's hot." I lowered my voice. "So what happens now?"

"Well," said Griffin, "Mendoza is going away for a while. Adam Hendricks has agreed to press charges so he's going down for kidnapping and assault at least. Sean's mother and her boyfriend are also pressing charges but we don't really need them to make the case. Probably just as well as I'm assuming you're going to press charges against the boyfriend for assault."

"Hell, yes," I said.

Griffin nodded approvingly. "Thanks to Sean's photos and a search we've done on Mendoza's house, he'll be going down on drugs charges. We've also got him on firearms charges. Mendoza's insisting he didn't kill Ryan Hendricks, but the situation now gives us enough reason to do a deeper investigation into the tox screen on his body. We can see if there is anything that we don't know about that's been injected in Ryan's system. Lucky for everyone involved, it looks like Mendoza's Uncle Johnny has decided he's too much trouble and maybe a stint in jail will do him some good. He's cutting him loose so there shouldn't be any threatened reprisals against anyone."

That was good. I really wanted to keep off the mobster's radar. My face throbbed.

"Man, this hurts," I said.

"A hit to the face always does." Griffin smiled, obviously remembering the one I had given him. I grinned at the memory.

"What's the smile for?" asked Griffin. I would have thought it looked more like a grimace considering how much my face hurt, but obviously Griffin had a different interpretation.

"I've got to say, a couple of years ago I would never have seen this happening to me."

"Why is that?" asked Griffin.

"Two years ago I was living in the town I was born in. I was engaged to my best friend. I was going to get married, have children and live in that town forever."

Griffin cocked an eyebrow. "Doesn't really sound like you."

"It was back then," I said reflectively.

"What happened?" asked Griffin.

"I got slapped up the side of the head with a dose of reality," I said, surprised to find the old note of bitterness in my voice. I really thought I had let it all go, obviously I hadn't. Griffin just sat there. He didn't push and I knew if I stopped talking he wouldn't press me for anymore.

"Paul was my best friend from when we were kids. We got engaged on my twenty first birthday. Paul and our life together was everything to me. I worked in a job I didn't really enjoy to save money for our future. A couple of years ago we went out with friends one night. I didn't want to go but it was expected that I would. I wanted to leave after a couple of hours but Paul wanted to stay. One of his friends offered to drive him home so I headed out early. On my way home a car coming the other way swerved and ran right into me. Found out the guy was drunk. I woke up in hospital a week later unable to feel my legs. I had some swelling near my spine. Everyone was hoping it would just be a mild bruising but at that stage no one knew if I was going to walk again. We hoped, but we didn't know. Paul wasn't there when I woke up. I asked for him and nobody would give me a direct answer as to where he was. A few days later Paul walked in with some flowers. It was obvious his family had made him come. Everyone left us alone and Paul told me that he was sorry but he didn't love me enough to be a full time caregiver for a cripple. That was the last I saw of him."

I looked over at Griffin and he looked angry. "What happened then?"

"I was one of the lucky ones," I said, smiling. "A few days later I started getting feeling back in my legs. I went into rehab and it took six months of work but I was able to walk again and then run again. While I was in the rehab center I took a good look at my life. I had lived my whole life towards the goal of marrying Paul. I had never actually taken the time to work out what I wanted, except for some silly dreams when I was a kid. That accident gave me the opportunity. I decided I wanted to travel. Took the insurance money from the accident and bought a ticket for London. Got some work there and met Monique, and that is why I am sitting in this interrogation room with an icepack on my face," I laughed ruefully.

"So this guy, Paul," Griffin growled, "ever speak to him or hear of him?"

I laughed. "Lord no, he lives in my home town but as far as my family is concerned he is dead to them. They don't mention his name. I have had no contact with him for two years."

"Still holding a candle for him?" Griffin asked insistently.

"No, strangely enough I think I grieved more for the life I lost than for him. I trusted him completely and he wasn't worth that trust. I won't say I don't have baggage from that mess but I'm not going to let it stop me living the life I want now."

A knock interrupted us and a uniformed cop poked his head through the door. "Sorry, Detective, but the old lady is getting a little bit antsy."

Great, Miss Betsy did not do inactivity well. I passed the icepack to Griffin.

"Thanks for that, I'd better get her and Sean home."

"What are you going to do with the kid?" Griffin asked.

"I'm not sure yet," I admitted. "I don't want him out on the streets and he can't go back to his mom. I think I'll talk to Reggie and see what our options are for him."

"He's lucky you found him. Not many kids in his position end up with someone who is willing to face down three guns for them."

I shrugged and headed to where Sean was drooling over Ramos. To give the poor woman credit she seemed to be embarrassed by the obvious adoration from the teenager. Grabbing his arm I dragged him to where Miss Betsy was haranguing some poor cop who looked barely older than Sean.

"Ready to go?" I asked.

"Do you know what this child is trying to do? He is trying to take my gun away from me."

Personally I was with the cop on this one. The more I saw Miss Betsy's attitude to that piece of metal, the more I was thinking that separating her from it was a good idea. Griffin came up and tapped the cop on the shoulder.

"That's okay, Miss Peterman, we've checked all your paperwork and it all seems to be in order."

"Of course it is," she said indignantly as she was handed her gun.

She then swept out of the station with Sean and me traveling in her wake. The drive back to the apartment complex was silent except for the quiet snores coming from Sean in the backseat. It seemed no matter what happened, a teenage boy could not be denied their sleep.

"So," said Miss Betsy, "your jerk of a fiancé ran out on you."

"How did you hear that?" I asked incredulously.

"They let me watch in the two way mirror. I was kind of hoping for a bit more action between you and the hot cop but I heard your story instead. Why did you never tell me about it? I told you everything about my bum of a husband."

"I don't know. I think I needed to put it far behind me. I didn't want to be that person again I guess. I never argued with Paul. Whatever he wanted, I did. I always wanted to keep the peace. When I look back on it I'm not particularly proud of the woman I was. The way I've spoken to Griffin, I would never have spoken to Paul like that."

"Griffin doesn't seem to mind, seems he likes the way you stand up to him."

"I don't know about that," I said, a slight blush creeping up my neck.

"One thing I will say, the bum hurt you years ago. Don't let him ruin your future as well, because he will if you let him."

"Is that what happened to you?" I asked.

"After I kicked out Lester, I was so bitter and hurt. There was a man, a good man who was a friend. I was so full of anger that I missed the opportunity that I could have had with him. Don't make the same mistake that I did. The best revenge you can get on the bum is to not let him damage you."

"Thank you," I said. "I'll try and remember that. If you do see me making that mistake feel free to kick me in the pants and remind me."

Miss Betsy laughed. "Don't think that I won't, missy, don't think that I won't." She was quiet for a moment as if making a decision. "So what are we going to do with the boy?" she asked, nodding her head in Sean's direction.

"I don't know. Do you think he could just stay with me

for a while?" I asked.

"You don't really have the room do you? He can't live on the couch forever."

"No, I guess not," I said quietly.

"Don't you worry about it dearie. Let me think on it for a bit and we'll work out something."

Chapter Twenty-One

Waking up late the next morning, I stumbled to the bathroom to get some painkillers. My face was throbbing painfully and I just wanted to get back in my bed and sleep the pain away. Knowing that wasn't a real possibility, I showered and got ready for the day. I walked out of the bathroom. Sean looked up at me and winced.

"Really," I said. "I can't look that bad."

"No, of course not," he said. "You look fine."

I looked at him sourly. "Little hint that will help you with all future dealings with women. You do not lie well. Either be completely honest or don't say anything."

"I'll take that advice on board," he said seriously.

"You do that," I chuckled.

Sean looked nervous.

"Okay buddy," I said. "Talk to me. There's obviously something you want to say."

"What you did for me yesterday, I don't know how to thank you. I feel like I should do something but I don't know what to do."

"Sean, I don't know what to say," I said. "Can't we just forget about it?"

"You don't understand," said Sean. "My mom would have left me to face that alone. She even told them when I walked in that they had me now, they should let her go. My mom did that. When he pointed that gun at my head, I figured who would care if I died if my own mom didn't. Then you walked in and saved my life by putting yours in danger. No one has ever done anything like that for me before. I don't know how to deal with it."

"Then don't," I said, as I started rattling plates and getting breakfast organized. "It's part of the past now.

Look at this as your second chance. What I want is for you to work out what you want to do with your life and chase after it. Live every moment of your life because now you know how amazing it is to be alive."

"You sound like you're talking from experience."

"I am," I said.

Sean got up and gave me a hug. "You're pretty awesome."

"Even though I'm not hot?" I teased.

"You are never going to let me forget that are you?" he said.

"No way, I am going to have that hanging over your head for the rest of your life."

The ringing of my phone interrupted us.

"Yes," I answered, still smiling at Sean.

"I need you to come and pick me up now. I am not staying in this place for one moment longer," the dulcet tones of Eleanor Channing came screeching down the phone.

I winced. I know that I hadn't held out much hope for her staying at the relaxation center for very long, but I had hoped she'd last longer than a couple of days.

"I'll be there as soon as I can," I said resignedly and hung up before she could start complaining. "Work's calling," I said to Sean. "I'll probably be out the rest of the day. If you need anything ask Miss Betsy."

"You're trusting me to stay alone in your home," said Sean.

"Sure, you've got a reason why I shouldn't?"

"No, just not many people would."

I shrugged as I stuck a piece of toast in my mouth.

Hurrying out, I knocked on Miss Betsy's door.

"I have to go to work," I said. "Could you please give Sean a hand if he needs it."

"Of course, sugar," she said smiling.

Driving up to the Happy Valley Relaxation Center, I found myself smiling. Sure I was driving to pick up one of the more annoying human beings on the planet and the chances that she had some illicit substances in her system were kind of high. Hopefully she was going to be mellow. Unfortunately, the way that my luck had been going lately, I wasn't thinking my chances were too good. Getting through security proved to be fun and by the time I actually got inside the center, I have to say my patience had been stretched as far as it could go.

This was not helped when Eleanor's first words to me were, "what took you so long?"

"Traffic," I snapped at her.

I organized the paperwork with a very grateful staff member and hustled Eleanor into the car.

"I need you to take me to Jennifer Saunders' house," she directed.

"Why on earth do you need to go there?" I asked.

"She contacted me and asked me to visit so we could sort out the lawsuit."

"Don't you think it would be better if you just left it to the lawyers?" I said.

"No, I heard that I missed out on getting a reading for that movie script I wanted because of my situation with Emily and Ryan. Emily's father is pulling some strings to screw me over."

"And you think suing his other daughter is the way to fix this." Sometimes I really wondered about people.

"No, but if I point out that I'm willing to drop the lawsuit if she has a word with her father..." she trailed off.

"Miss Channing, there is a reason that you pay a lot of money to your lawyers and manager. Don't you think that this kind of negotiation would be better left to them?"

"No, Jennifer wants to talk to me. Besides it'll do that family good to have to beg for once."

I concentrated on the road. Sometimes I seriously dislike the people that I work for and this would be one of those moments. I liked Jennifer Saunders. I didn't want to have to watch her beg to an entitled diva like Eleanor

Channing.

Jennifer greeted us at the front door with an effusive smile.

"Thank you so much for coming, I'm really hoping that we can work this situation out and put the unpleasantness behind us."

"There wouldn't be any unpleasantness if your father and sister would put aside the situation with Ryan," Eleanor said sweetly.

I was beginning to feel ill. I felt sorry for Jennifer. With Eleanor's star power, she could crush Jennifer's business with one Twitter rant.

"I think we can work this out," I said, trying to be the peacemaker yet again.

Eleanor didn't look convinced.

"Maybe a business collaboration," Jennifer ventured. "We are currently releasing an organic fruit and vegetable detox cleansing diet. I'm sure we could work out a campaign between us that puts you front and center. All natural, all organic. In fact why don't you try some?"

Jennifer busied herself in the kitchen juicing the vegetables and I sat next to Eleanor.

"I'm bored," she complained. I struggled not to roll my eyes.

"You are the one who wanted to come here," I said, exasperated at this sudden change in mood.

"Only because I wanted to see what Ryan saw in her," she said as she picked at the fabric on the couch.

"Ryan was engaged to Emily," I reminded her.

"Well yes, but he was sleeping with Jennifer first."

"But she's married," I said, my jaw dropping.

Eleanor simply looked at me like I was an idiot, and you know what, I kind of had to agree with her. I was an idiot. I was reminded of my visit here and the way Jennifer had spoken about her husband, as if he wasn't really present in the marriage anymore. Lonely, neglected wife with a husband caught up in his activism. I could see why falling for sexy Ryan Hendricks would be easy to do.

"Here we are," announced Jennifer as she walked back in the room. Passing a glass to Eleanor and me, she smiled. "To better understanding," she said and started drinking from her own glass.

Eleanor brought the drink to her lips and took a sip. "That's really not bad," she said, taking a second sip.

As I raised the glass to my lips, my phone rang and I saw that it was Griffin.

Putting the glass down, I said, "I'm sorry, I've got to take this." Stepping through the large doors at the back of the house, I answered the phone as I looked out over the national park that came up to the back of the property.

"Hi," I said, feeling a bit tongue tied.

"Hi," said Griffin.

There was silence.

"Can I help you with something?" I asked.

Griffin cleared his throat. "Uh yeah, I just thought I'd let you know that they've done further testing on Ryan Hendricks and they found something."

"A new drug?" I asked.

"No," he said. "It seems that Ryan Hendricks died of oleander poisoning. Oleander is a plant that grows naturally. It's actually pretty common."

"I know what oleander is," I said. "There was some on the farm when I was growing up and it poisoned some of the sheep. My dad and I had to dig it out."

"Yeah well, this stuff is nasty. It can poison you just by being on your skin. We don't know yet how it got into Ryan."

A sick feeling started in the bottom of my stomach.

"Griffin," I said, lowering my voice. "I am currently standing on the rear porch of a house that backs onto national park. I was here a few days ago and the park has oleander bushes growing near the fence."

"Are you sure?" he asked.

"I almost sprained my wrist pulling out those plants at

home. Believe me I know what they look like and I am looking at a bush that is about fifteen feet high, growing over the fence just in front of me."

"Trudie, they are everywhere. It's a common plant in LA. What makes you think that these are the oleander bushes that poisoned Ryan?" Griffin asked patiently.

"Because I am standing in Jennifer Saunders' house. Jennifer's company supplies an organic diet juice that I saw in Ryan's refrigerator, which means he was drinking it before his death. Did you know that Jennifer was sleeping with Ryan until he left her for her sister?"

I looked through the door and saw Jennifer pouring more juice into Eleanor's glass.

"Griffin," I said, moving quickly. "I need you to get here right now. I think Jennifer is trying to poison Eleanor Channing."

As Eleanor raised the glass again, I raced inside and grabbed hold of it, put it rather forcefully on the coffee table and grabbed Eleanor's arm.

"I'm sorry," I said, with a forced smile on my lips. "That was just a phone call from Eleanor's manager. We need to get to a meeting with him right away."

"No we don't," Eleanor said.

"Yes we do," I said, forcefully gripping her arm, pulling her towards the front door.

"I don't think you should leave just now," said Jennifer and I heard an ominous click behind us.

Turning around, I saw Jennifer and for the second time in twenty-four hours, I had a gun pointed straight at me.

"Jennifer," I said quietly. "What are you doing?"

"You know, don't you?" she said.

"I don't know anything Jennifer," I said as calmly as I could. "I just need to get Eleanor home."

"Why do you care? She's a horrible person. Just like Emily. They don't care who they hurt."

Eleanor had finally worked out that keeping her mouth shut was the best course of action.

"Ryan loved me," Jennifer said. "He made me happy. Do you know how long it's been since someone made me happy? All Josh cares about is his causes. He doesn't even see me anymore. Ryan saw me."

"What happened?" I asked.

"Emily found out about us and just because I had him, she went after him. She's been like that ever since we were kids. The main reason I married Josh is because he was never interested in Emily. I didn't work out until later that he wasn't really interested in me either. Ryan fell for it, just like every other guy. He left me and got engaged to her."

I nodded. No way did I want to say anything that was going to set the unhinged woman with the gun off. I was ready to elbow Eleanor if she so much as took an intake of breath, because nothing that came out of that mouth was going to help our situation.

"She was always throwing it in my face, that she took him away from me, that he wanted her more. And then he was sleeping with so many other women. Why wasn't I enough?"

Seeing the tears in her eyes, I couldn't help but feel sorry for her. Of course, feeling sorry for her didn't negate what I thought she'd done to Eleanor.

"You poisoned Ryan didn't you?" I asked as gently as I could.

Jennifer nodded. "I couldn't let Emily have him."

"Jennifer, have you given Eleanor some of that poison?"

Again Jennifer nodded. Eleanor gasped and went to step forward but I used that elbow to good effect.

"I need to get Eleanor to a hospital, Jennifer," I said.

"No," said Jennifer, her resolve suddenly stiffening and the gun which had started to lower was once again pointing at us. "She was trying to steal Ryan away from Emily. She's just as bad as Emily is. I can't hurt Emily, she's my sister, but I can get rid of Eleanor."

"Please, Jennifer, don't do this," I pleaded, my eyes

firmly on the gun.

"I have to," she said, and I could see her swing the gun towards Eleanor.

Eleanor screamed and as I went to push her out of the way, I felt a searing pain in my right side and then nothing.

Chapter Twenty-Two

Opening my eyes had never seemed to be such a monumental task before. My eyelids felt like they were stuck together and all I could hear was beeping.

"I think she's waking up, get a doctor." I heard Griffin's voice and even feeling as bad as I did, it still went right through me.

The bright light as my eyelids opened seemed to pierce through my brain and it took me a second to focus. I saw Griffin's tired unshaven face looking down at me.

"Don't you ever do anything like that again," he growled.

"Yelling at her is probably not being helpful," said a large nurse as she shoved Griffin out of the way. "Now you ignore him, honey," she said soothingly. "Men have a tendency to get a bit growly when their women do something stupid like step in front of a bullet."

"I was shot?" I croaked. How the hell did I accomplish that?

"What was the last thing you remember?" she asked.

"I was talking to Jennifer. She pointed the gun at Eleanor and I went to push Eleanor out of the way. Are you telling me I took a bullet for that woman?" I said in disgust.

"Yes sunshine, you did. On behalf of those who have been working her ward, we really want to know what on Earth was going through that head of yours."

I tried to shrug my shoulders, only to get a shooting pain go through my side.

"What happened?" I looked around at my room and saw that not only was Griffin standing there, but also Miss Betsy had managed to find herself a chair. Sean seemed to be camped out on the floor in the corner.

"I need everyone out," said the doctor as he strode into the room.

Miss Betsy put her arm around Sean's shoulders and hustled him out of the room, ignoring the mutinous look on his face. Griffin gave me a look that I had no idea how to interpret before heading out.

"I'll be just outside," he said.

Finally given some peace I took stock of my situation. I wiggled all my fingers and toes. Okay, they were all working. My side though was burning with pain.

"What happened?" I asked.

"You caught a bullet in your right side. You were lucky though. It hit your rib and got deflected out. Your rib is cracked underneath the bullet wound. That was relatively minor."

"Really, doc, and how many minor bullet wounds have you had?" I said sarcastically.

The doctor stopped. "Point taken. I meant that it was minor compared to the concern we had when you fell. You hit your head and you've been unconscious for three days."

Okay, I could see where the priority was now. He checked my eyes with a light and asked some questions. When he appeared satisfied with my answers, I asked him whether I could get up.

The doctor looked at me strangely.

"If I can get up, go to the bathroom and brush my teeth, I know I'll be okay," I explained.

He nodded and motioned for the nurse to help me. In the bathroom I found the toiletries pack and, keeping a tight grip on the sink, I brushed my teeth. The nurse leaned against the wall and watched me. I looked in the mirror and noted the white bandage patch on my forehead. I lifted my shirt and found another bandage around my middle.

"Because the bullet deflected it came out again," the

nurse said. "A bit of a messy through and through. You've already had a plastic surgeon work on it. Some woman organized it saying she would never convince you to wear a bikini if you had that scar there."

I nodded. "That would be my boss, Monique."

"You've got good people around you," the nurse said. "The waiting room is full and that cop of yours hasn't left your side."

"He's a friend," I said.

"Girl," she said, as I leaned on her while we were walking out of the bathroom. "Believe me, I've been here the last three days and that man is not just a friend."

She was chuckling as I got back into bed.

"Are you ready to face everyone?" she said.

I looked down at myself. "I'm not exposing anything I shouldn't?" I asked.

"No, sweetie, you're not," she said with a smile.

The first one through the door was Crystal and I think she may have body checked Edwin as they came through. Behind them was Miss Betsy and Sean with Monique. Right at the back I was surprised to see Jorge. Griffin was there as well but he hung back. After assuring everyone I was okay I discovered that things had moved along while I was unconscious. Jennifer was in jail awaiting trial. It seemed that not even her father's influence could get her out of this mess. Eleanor had been brought to hospital with oleander poisoning and her stomach had been pumped, an experience that she had felt the need to share with everyone according to Jorge. Before long the nurse came back and told everyone to leave. Crystal and Edwin left, promising to see me first thing in the morning.

Monique kissed my cheek and with tears in her eyes whispered in my ear. "I am so happy you are healthy, ma petite."

Miss Betsy dragged a not happy Sean out after she promised him that they would be back the next day. Jorge came up to the bed and kissed me on the cheek.

"Get better soon, cupcake," he said. "I've missed you at work."

Griffin's eyes darkened at the action and Jorge kept his eyes on Griffin as he sauntered out. Griffin walked over and sat on the bed.

"Aren't you going too?" I asked.

"Nope, special dispensation. Police protection."

"I thought she was in jail. What exactly are you protecting me from?"

"I'll think of something," he said, smiling.

I sobered quickly. "So what really happened?"

"Jennifer Saunders had an affair with Ryan Hendricks. When he ended it and started seeing her sister she got jealous. We tested that detox concoction in his refrigerator and there was enough oleander to kill him in that easily. You were right, there were oleander bushes all along the back fence of their home in the national park. At some point someone thought it would make a great screening plant to hide the house from hikers. One of the scientists even found poison in the honey from their bee hives."

"Eleanor's skin reaction," I said.

"It looks like she got a small dose when she had the milk and honey bath at Bliss. Since the story has gone out there have been a couple of other people who've come forward with the same reaction."

"Did anyone eat the honey?" I asked.

"No. Fortunately it hadn't been approved for human consumption yet."

"Did Jennifer know about the honey?" I asked.

"No," said Griffin. "Neither did the husband. He was pretty messed up about the bees. Strangely enough he was more upset about that than he was about the fact that his wife had been having an affair and murdered someone."

"Poor Jennifer," I murmured.

Griffin looked at me strangely.

"I'm not saying I agree with what she did, but look at how the people who were supposed to love and care about her treated her. Her husband barely noticed her and her sister stole away the only happiness she found."

"You have got the biggest heart of anyone I know," Griffin said. "You might want to hold off on the sympathy a bit. The glasses of juice she gave to you and Eleanor had enough oleander in it that you would have both been dead within a day. As it was we barely got Eleanor to the hospital in time."

"What happened?"

"I got to the house and was coming through the door when I heard the shot. Luckily I think she was so surprised that it was you who had caught the bullet and not Eleanor that I was able to tackle and disarm her. At that point we had cops and an ambulance there. Eleanor had run, leaving you to die when the gun fired."

I could tell by the way Griffin's mouth tightened that he wasn't happy with that.

"The cops found her on her hands and knees, vomiting on the front lawn."

Now there was a lovely image.

"Once I'd taken Jennifer out of the picture, I put pressure on your wound and came to the hospital with you in the ambulance. I've been here ever since."

I put my hand against his cheek, rough with whiskers.

"You stayed with me," I said.

He leaned towards me, his lips barely brushing mine.

"I wanted to be here when you woke up," he whispered.

A tear slid down my cheek and he brought his hand up and brushed it from my face. Gently he pressed his lips against mine, my face cupped in his hands. My eyes fluttered shut and I felt the strength and the softness of his lips as they moved over mine. Increasing the pressure I felt his tongue flick against the seam of my lips and I parted them and he deepened the kiss.

"What the hell are you doing to my daughter?"

I wrenched myself away.

"Mom," I croaked.

"Mom," Griffin repeated, snapping out of the kiss haze we had been in.

Sure enough, there was my mother standing next to Reggie in the doorway, ready to protect and do battle for her firstborn. She was looking at Griffin with the same look in her eyes that she had when four year old Alan Vaughan pushed me over in kindergarten. Reggie looked apologetically at me. Obviously he had filled my mother in on Griffin's role in my life. Griffin had a panicked look on his face, and if he had been a lesser man I was sure he would have bolted. In fact, he still might.

Once again my mother had managed to destroy any chance of one of her children having a love life with no effort at all. It was like it was her superpower.

"So, what's this I hear about you managing to get yourself shot?" My mother glared at me.

Of course, because this was all my fault.

Mom sat down on the bed and patted my leg.

"That's okay, Trudie, I'm going to stay with you until you're all better," she said, looking at Griffin balefully. "I'm not going to let anyone hurt my baby girl again."

Griffin looked over her head at me. I could see that he was trying to work out if that had been a threat or a promise. He needn't have bothered. I knew my mother. It was a threat.

About The Author

Leonie Gant started her writing career at the age of ten when she stuffed notes in her pencil case full of ideas for mysteries that Nancy Drew and the Hardy Boys should really have been solving. After years of watching mysteries play out in her head, she decided that writing them down was the best way to deal with them.

In her life away from writing, she is a voracious reader with not nearly enough time to make her way through all the books that she wants to read. She enjoys bushwalking, sewing and chocolate, possibly not in that order. She also believes in the value of trying new things, walking in the rain and enjoying every moment.

To find out more about Leonie Gant and her books
www.leoniegant.com

Discover other titles by Leonie Gant
Not Happily Married in Hollywood
Not Talented in Hollywood
Not Wanted in Hollywood
Not Suspicious in Hollywood
Not Forgotten in Hollywood